29.95

Bes
1990

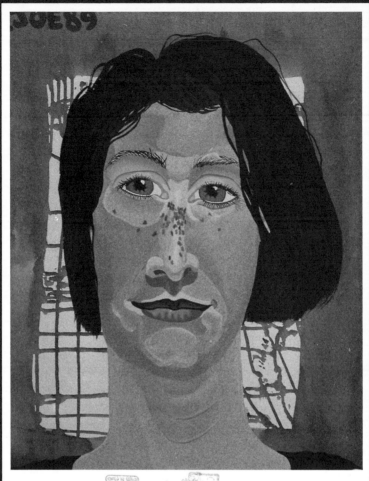

**90** Best Canadian Stories

Edited by David Helwig & Maggie Helwig

# Introduction

And so, once again, here I am, your friendly compere (strange British use of a French word), your master of ceremonies, host, your Mr. Interlocutor (does anyone remember minstrel shows?) to present the annual revue of high-wire acts, dancing bears, clowns, marketplace mythmakers, bar-room anecdotalists, tap-dancing punsters, ancient mariners, gossips, gospellers, historians, wise old women, bedtime comforters and accomplished liars, all this gang of storytellers who have designs on your heart and soul.

Who else but Timothy Findley knew about the duel? Who else but Leon Rooke heard the stories about the disappearing children? Who else but Linda Svendsen knew the real meaning of the atom bomb? Who else but Rohinton Mistry knew the glitter of the marbles in the moonlight?

How, somebody says, do you know they're the best stories? The very best? Well, one way is what I said, that each is a story no-one else knew, that was a secret from the beginning of the world until now.

As usual, the book contains stories by those who have been doing tricks for years and stories by those who are just beginning to be noticed subway busking in the little magazines.

Turn a page and a curtain will open on well-furnished rooms, lost empires, hidden villages, hints about the past. Brain transfusions.

Have some.

DAVID HELWIG

Contributions for the twenty-first volume, published or unpublished, should be sent to the editors, David Helwig and Maggie Helwig, at 106 Montreal Street, Kingston, Ontario K7K 3E8 before 30 November, 1990. All manuscripts should be accompanied by a stamped self-addressed envelope.

# Stardust

**Linda Svendsen**

In the biggest little city in the World, back in 1954, everybody blamed the A-bomb. Betty Crocker cakes falling in
the oven. Singing flat. Winners losing life savings at black-
jack, shimmy, craps and the one-armed bandits in carpet
joints on Virginia. Goats turning blue. Divorcees-to-be
changing minds over night and flying back east, and brides
with headaches that wouldn't go away. It took longer for the
sun to set, and get up again. One night it rained cactus
needles in downtown Reno. The mayor wouldn't declare a

7

disaster area. They dropped one off a tower in Yucca Flats, another out of a B-52 over what would be called the Proving Grounds, and out of the blue, Dad asked if I wanted to view a test. He knew somebody.

We lived in a stucco duplex around the corner from the Chapel of the Silver Bells. Dad was on call. Occasionally the pastor phoned in the middle of the night, and Dad would throw on a shirt and antelope cufflinks and tux, and rush over to perform "Oh What a Beautiful Mornin'!" or "The Lord is My Shepherd" or "Witchcraft" or "There's No Business Like Show Business," and collect 25 big buckeroos. Witnessing was an additional five, and Mum sometimes subbed for Dad if he was out of town, or at the Stardust, or had laryngitis. Both wept admirably at weddings, dabbing the perpetual handkerchief against a cheek; this made brides blush and grooms generous. Mum and Dad used to rehearse crying and mornings I could stroll into our sunny kitchen, alive with the smell of bacon, and find them in tears at the table.

Big Eddie Brookmore, my Dad, he'd always sung. Said he was shot not kicking, crooning, out of his mother's womb and had never shut up. Back in West New York, New Jersey, when another teacher needed a baritone, Big Eddie was borrowed from gym class or trig, and when the army acknowledged Brookmore couldn't aim and shoot, they put him in the chorus, and when Dad was discharged, he hustled to Hollywood to sing for his supper, lunch, breakfast. But he didn't have the Sinatra family connections, the agent of an Allen Jones, the luck of a Como. Daytime he sang radio jingles for Singer vacuums and cold cream; nights he had a gig on an illegal gambling ship cruising three miles off the coast of Southern California. With the circus he toured Washington, Nevada, Oregon and British

8

Columbia, and eloped with the spinster Lucy Birch, and when the casinos finally docked permanently in the desert, my Dad, already a big fish in the Biggest Little City, welcomed old buddy pit bosses and the fixed wheels of chance.

My Dad wasn't tall, but his booming voice lent the illusion of height and, more importantly, power. His mission was to make certain listeners hear the words. Consonants counted, t's were ticked off, so when he sang "Mares eat oat, and does eat oats, and little lambs eat ivy," the crowd knew who ate what. He was good-looking in a hairy sort of way, with a belly he was always going to 86, and lips so shiny pink that ladies stopped to seek an autograph, then his beauty secret. Did he apply anything special? The scar over his right eye reminded me of the pale trail of a slug. He'd gotten it when he was twelve, playing the lead in a Gilbert and Sullivan operetta, and had been butted by a swabman's mop. But he looked you in the eye, and was blond, full of breath and himself, we both thought he was A-1.

Dad did the anthem at the baseball game, and when we were already down in the third inning, he collected his cash and we took off in his friend the coach's Cadillac. We cruised out of town, past Sparks, following the Truckee River as long as it paralleled the road. This was the route we took to go fishing at Pyramid Lake. We sped by cowblinders, and what I called cow-udder cactus, and saguaros my Dad said stuck up like a man's stiff dong in the AM. Then we made a sharp right and drove seven hours straight south all the way to Jackass Flats. Dad was keen on seeing history go up in smoke and kept saying so.

We didn't talk much. I pulled caps off Rainier beers, Dad drained them, and the brown bottles rolled and clinked under my feet. Occasionally Dad would quit guzzling, and burst into a verse of "The Lady is a Tramp" or "Yes, We Have No Bananas" or "Blue Skies," then he'd wink at me and say, "Take it Away, Sunray," and, waving my pointer fingers, I'd conduct an invisible combo, bop my head and grin like a loon. Sometimes we'd pull over on the shoulder and take long leaks on our own long shadows. My father and I were close that trip. He didn't need to pitch a curve ball, and I didn't stretch out of my skin to catch something falling fast out of the sky.

We stayed at the Alamo Motel in a little hole-in-the-wall an hour from our final destination. Dad tuned in the Giants and the Red Sox, and we finished up some stale chicken sandwiches and warm beer in front of the radio, and we called that happy, even when the Giants got licked and we called it a day. The last thing my father said, before conking out in the double, was, "What you going to be? If yu grow up," and I said, from the couch, "I reckon you."

The next morning we pulled into a fenced chunk of desert and Dad leaned on one elbow, out the window, to talk to a soldier in what looked like a tollbooth. The sign said, "United States Army. Restricted Entry." Dad gave his name and added. "Guests of Colonel Frazier's." The soldier, who didn't look a lot older than me, ran down a list with his finger, shook his head, and went up it. Then he turned his head away and barked into the walkie-talkie. Dad put the Caddy into park, shut her off and looked straight ahead, strictly business, at the hills.

I had a funny feeling we weren't going to get past the gate. It didn't matter. I just didn't want to hear Dad argue with the soldier, or demand to talk to Colonel Frazier directly or, worse, be hangdog, or still worse, shout the highlights of his life in uniform and how he belted his guts out for his brothers in green. I started to sweat under my collar and stared at the little Cadillac crown on the glove compartment. Then the soldier stuck a ticket under the wiper-blade and said, "Proceed."

Dad started the car and threw his hands against his forehead in a form of salute. "You're going to like Colonel Frazier, Ray," he said. "Me and him and the Bugs, Jesus H. Christ, we used to paint the town." By Bugs, he meant Bugsy Siegel, and I never quite believed Dad and the gambling boss had been bosom buddies to the extent of winning and wining, bedding and dining, sisters. If he'd been so close to Siegel, we should have been a Flamingo family. Why weren't we living high off the hog in Vegas? He geared down. In a few minutes, the car hugged curves and we climbed in silence. It was almost as if Dad had heard me thinking.

At the top of the mountain we parked behind a jeep. Ladies, probably officer's wives, were gussied up in poodle skirts or suitdresses, and clutching white patent purses against white patent belts cinched to the last notch. We walked behind their rhythm hips, and wall of cologne and chatter. Their hair didn't budge in the breeze. Dad opened the lookout door for them.

"Thank you," one said

"Nice day to die," the sunglasses gal joked. Her hair hung long; she looked like Veronica Lake, only brunette.

"Indeed." Dad winked. Mr. Debonair.

We were in a rustic cabin with about 30 others, mostly army brass and guests and personnel. Colonel Frazier wasn't there and a sergeant didn't know why. "Maybe overslept," he said giddily. There were huge urns of coffee, and open boxes of fancy iced doughnuts from a bakery in Las Vegas; and a map of Nevada with my favourite towns

Searchlight and Lovelock and Contact, and a blackboard covered with math; and radios, telescopes, clocks with five hands, and such, and big thick windows looking out on nothing but sagebrush and blue skies. The lookout atmosphere wasn't unlike fellowship after Sunday service. We underwent another identification procedure and Dad, performing for the ladies now, said he was born in Lower Slobovia and actually got a titter.

A major general spoke briefly before the countdown. He told us from what height the bomb would drop, who was flying, and how this stacked up to Fat Man and Little Boy, and that the worst damage might be a blazing prairie dog and wouldn't that be God's blessing? We were five miles from ground zero. We put on the intensity goggles. I looked sideways at Dad, looking at the brunette, who was between sunglasses and goggles. I couldn't tell the colour of her eyes. Then we bowed our heads for a quick prayer and heard the command, "Bomb away."

The sun looked like an old dime. I looked for anything, for a parachute bursting open, for a jet zooming toward Idaho. The desert stayed dull, and 30 seconds had gone by, the doughnuts were right behind me, and I thought the bomb was a dud. Then the sky heaved inside out and turned green as a new pool table. The ladies gasped. Fire, like a spitball reversed, soared back up where it had come from. A dust cloud three miles long spread every which way. In my teeth and balls, behind my eyes, I felt heat where I'd never before. The crowd applauded the shaky mushroom and Dad looked around, looking like he might commemorate the occasion with a patriotic melody. But he didn't. He took hold of my arm during the shock wave, whether to steady himself or me, I couldn't tell, and he flashed a smile. Then we watched six jets streak into the black cloud and disappear.

Isobel was the brunette's name. Her favourite song was "How Much is that Doggie in the Window?" by Patti Page, and she could bark just like the pooch on the record, and had no qualms about doing so in public. Her voice was deep. She wasn't married to an officer; she was lingering in Vegas for a divorce. This was her fifth week and she had one to go. She hailed from Rehobeth Beach, in Delaware, and her husband owned a chain of laundromats, which were big business on the east coast, where people lived in tiny closets overflowing with dirty clothes. She wasn't sad about getting divorced, or if she was, it didn't show. She was impressed that Dad was an artist, asked if I was an only child, and said I was tough as a weed, and tall, for nine.

At the lookout she'd asked for a ride to Vegas; her friend, an officer's wife, was going on to a post-bomb blast at the officer's mess. Isobel didn't feel well. She thought it might be radiation sickness, but the readings didn't agree. Dad said we were heading south, which was news to me, and that she was welcome to join us. We had lots of room.

Isobel and Dad talked all the way to town, and when we pulled up in front of her boarding-house, she invited us in for supper. She didn't seem sick anymore. She was full of beans, in my opinion. The rooming-house was Spanish, with a big fireplace, and tall dark furniture, and white walls and posters of mad bulls charging matadors. Two other divorcees-to-be also roomed there, and Isobel introduced them. Susan was younger than Isobel, maybe nineteen, and looked as if she'd been born crying. Nina was the other. She asked us how we liked the bomb. She'd been caught in the flash while doing her toe-touches and the patio had shook. She also mentioned they'd felt the blast in Texas because her husband had called from Dallas to inquire if she'd died or anything. Dad and I stayed for pork chops and then stayed overnight. I asked if we should call Mum, but Dad seemed to think she'd guess we were staying with Colonel Frazier, or at a motel, and wouldn't worry.

I slept in an empty divorcee's room. From the window I could see the hot lights of the strip. The hundred winking bulbs of a horseshoe, the neon tip of a ten-gallon cowboy hat, the words JACKPOT and LUCKY and 21 flashing off and on. I thought about wandering around, or waking up Dad and driving all night back to Reno, and Mum, and our own beds. He was sleeping on the black leather couch in the living-room.

I pulled my dungarees on, and shirt, opened the door and groped my way down the hall. Somebody was in the bathroom; there was a wedge of light under the door and I heard somebody crying. Probably Susan. I made it into the living-room, found the outline of the couch and felt for Dad's shoulder, Dad's back. He wasn't there. I pulled the blanket right off the couch. I said, "Dad?" and then tripped over his Italian wingtips. He couldn't have gone far.

Although it was close to dawn, the house was dark. I listened for breathing, for footsteps, for whoever had been crying. The headlights of a turning car swept the living-room, and the car picked up speed going down the street. I could hear crickets rubbing their legs together. I headed into the kitchen and looked out the screen door.

Dad smoked a cigarette out on the patio. He sat at a picnic table, talking with his hands. She sat across from him. She wasn't saying anything, she was nodding, she was looking at him. He reached over and took her hand. He leaned across the table and she leaned toward him. Then they both got up and walked to the Cadillac in the driveway. I remember thinking that he couldn't go anywhere, he couldn't go without me, his shoes were by the couch in the living-room, how could he drive without shoes? But they got in and they didn't go any place I could see.

On my way back to my room, I bumped into Isobel coming out of the bathroom. "Oh, you," she said. "You having trouble sleeping?"

I said I was. Maybe too much excitement, which was what Mum always said before Sports Day, or the Fourth of July, or Christmas.

"That test riled me," Isobel said. "I have this feeling the world's going to end, or something."

I looked toward her one eye, the other being hidden by that long sweep of bang, and nodded.

My mother loved to remember how she fell in love with my father, left her country and family, and followed her heart. She remembered it when she matched and folded socks, when she witnessed weddings at the Silver Bells, when Dad crooned "Yessir, That's My Baby," as she walked into a room with dry cleaning or Nanaimo bars or what-have-you. Sometimes during those sad spells in the marriage, when she slipped into bed by his sleeping body, and only had the dark to hold onto, she held onto that memory. I know this because she told me. She told me one night when she'd been downing highballs and didn't think I understood anyway, being a boy. (She'd read about the arc of passion in *True Story.* There might have been an article by that name, or maybe she'd been drinking and it was "Ache" or "Ark," I don't know. The main thing was she traced this in her life with Dad. It worried her no end.)

You have to picture her. Strict Dutch parents with beds

in separate bedrooms, the oldest of four daughters, strapped to a piano before and after school. Playing for assemblies and church led her down the garden path to tea dances and Sadie Hawkins' social and bottle clubs, and taking the tram home at eleven with a rowdy crowd. Her heart broken when the violinist next door died of influenza and her father saying, "There's more fish in the sea, Lucy dear. More fish." The same little girl who had glanced out the window during history and had whispered, amazed, "It's snowing," because it only ever rains in Vancouver, and had been made to stand in front of the class and say, "It's snowing," one hundred times, this was my mother.

It was the old story of the circus pitching its tent in town. It was the old story of the mysterious fair stranger, who knows the can-can, and the shy spinster dying to do it. Mum swore the Tattooed Lady, with whom she shared a dressing-room and hair spray, introduced them. Dad claimed it was the senile magician. It didn't matter. They would have met anyway with the same result. She had to play his act in his key; she had to learn his cues; she had to marry him to beget me. She was born to be billed a hussy by her parents and fall, at 30, for Eddie Brookmore.

I've seen a picture of them eating Chinese food with the circus folks. They must have worked together a few times by then. Their faces are scrubbed, sensitive, like kids' after Hallowe'en and they're in a big booth at the Ho Inn. Mum's holding a fork between a bowl of rice and her mouth, and nothing's on it. She's smiling at Dad, who's next to her. He's got an arm over a shoulder and beams to the left of the camera. The Tattooed Lady is in the middle of a slap, or she's caressing his arm. (I could never make out her designs, but Dad said she had a nice peacock and her body resembled a zoo.) He's pincered a fortune cookie with his chopsticks and lifted it up, as if saying, "What have we here?" I'd pay dough to know what it said inside.

Years later when I asked Mum how she found out, she crossed her arms and said, "Put two and two together."

She said Dad had put a down payment on a car and worked Vegas every other weekend. She said he sang in a side lounge in one of the carpet joints and he said the cheque made it worth his drive. She said he called Reno one-horse and I remember that, too. He did 50 push-ups, raising his hands off the floor and clapping for 25, and refused sour cream on his baked potato. He sacked out late. Mum always had to reach for his hand, tilt her head, and say, "Can I have a kiss?" This was only a month after the detonation. She wasn't stupid. Even if Dad wasn't admitting anything, she could read my unhappy face.

Over Sunday breakfast she said, "Eddie, why don't you take Ray to Vegas with you next weekend? There's that big car show."

Dad concentrated on his pancakes. He chopped at a pat of frozen butter.

"I don't care if I go," I said.

"You like cars."

"Don't like Vegas," I said.

She looked over at Dad, and Dad said, "You do so. Like Vegas."

Mum stared at me.

"It's okay," I said. "I don't want to go to the car show, that's all. They're boring. You have to line up to look under a hood. You'll be busy."

"Your father isn't too busy to take you. Are you hon?"

"I'm not prepared to take somebody who doesn't want to go," Dad said.

"You come too then, Mum," I said. She watched Dad carefully pour a capful of maple syrup over his stack. Neither of them said anything further.

The next day Mum held the scissors over my head in the kitchen. She had Ed Sullivan in mind; I wanted a "Dragnet" cut, something Joe Friday to impress the guys at school. I liked the feeling of my hair pulled taut between her two fingers, and the itchy-sounding scrape of the shears as she cut straight across. She walked around me and I caught a faint whiff of Wild Turkey. She sometimes bent my head slightly, and I'd stare at a square of linoleum lighter than the others, at a plaque of a banana holding hands with an apple, or at things I'd never noticed before. When she was done, we walked to the bathroom mirror and she held up another one behind me.

"I'm bald."

"Don't be dramatic."

"You've scalped me."

Mum brushed her hand across the top. "It'll be cool. You have a nice neck."

"Nobody wants to look at necks all day."

"I want your hair short for when we visit your grandparents," Mum said. "And I don't want to hear boo." She walked back to the kitchen and started sweeping up my hair.

I fetched the dustpan. "Since when are we going?"

"Since I don't know," Mum said.

"Does Dad know?"

Mum let go of the broom and it clattered to the floor. She grabbed my chin. "Do *you* know?" she asked sharply. "Do you? Does everybody?" When she realized she was hurting me, she let go, and headed outside. I crawled on my hands and knees to the front door and cracked open our letter slot. She sat, her back to me and the house, on our single step in the hot sun. I couldn't see all of her.

Friday nights Mum popped corn and we tried to reach an agreement over who got to watch what channel. She could watch "Coke Time with Eddie Fisher," if I got the last half-hour of "Rin Tin Tin." I liked "Ozzie and Harriet," and we both loved "Topper," especially Neil, the silly St. Bernard. (We both liked shows with dogs, but Mum was always partial to shows with singers. They beat dogs in her books.) At nine, she played "Dollar a Second," and then, for her bonus, watched "Our Miss Brooks," and then the rest of the night was all mine, with "Gillette Cavalcade of Sports" and "Great Moments in Sports," and Mumbo, the sport, took a vinegar bath, then read *Reader's Digest* or copied recipes from cookbooks onto ruled cards, or wandered in to fiddle with the rabbit ears and find a clearer picture.

That night Mr. Fisher had just finished his theme, "May I Sing to You," when Mum walked in with two suitcases and an overnight grip, put them down by the front door, and phoned a taxi. She gave our address. She added that we were right behind the Silver Bells. Then she hung up, and we looked at each other. "What?" I said.

"Get your coat," she said. "It might be chilly."

The Stardust had penny slots and a T-bone steak special, which kept the joint jumping. We knew everybody—pit bosses, shills, dice boys, the part-time keno caller, cowpokes and wheel-rollers, the chef, everybody except the out-of-towners and lapsed Mormons. It was one big navy-blue room, with navy-blue carpet climbing halfway up the walls; with chandeliers, stars, smoke and mirrors stuck on the ceiling; and everywhere the chime of coins, and shuffling decks, and lighters clicking, and fortunes sliding easily back and forth over green felt. Gamblers concentrated so fierce they didn't swallow or blink.

She left our luggage with Bill the bellhop. Then she dug into her purse, opened her wallet, and handed me two tens. "I'll be over there. Bring me some nickels."

When I joined her at the slots, she had already fed the machine and was shaking its hand again. She showed a melon and orange, a bell and bar, and a plum. She kept the plum. She pulled again, and got a bell, a seven. She kept the seven, pulled again, and got a bell and a melon. "Should have kept bells," she said.

"Black Jack, Mum."

She shook her head. "I've only played once."

"Doesn't matter. You'll have an edge against the house."

Mum looked tired. She was dressed in a skirt with bars of music and treble clefs, a blouse, and black cardigan, and held onto a blue plastic bucket brimming with silver. "What time is it?" she said.

"Ten past nine."

"We've got half an hour."

She cased the room, and then headed toward Jimmy the croupier's roulette wheel. "Hey, Jimmy," she said, and didn't look back. She bet odd, and won. She bet even, red even, black even, black odd, red odd, a couple of splits, a straight, a street and a square, and a low baker's dozen. Jimmy asked after my Dad and I made a face, so he asked us what we'd like to drink. Mum had brandy chasers; I nursed Dr. Pepper. By the time we grabbed our bags, and ran into the Greyhound station to board the northbound bus, Mum was drunk, and flush, and even with America.

It was raining when we reached Klamath Falls, Oregon, and almost light. My mother had told me our plan. Dad would return from his fling in Vegas with that homewrecker and find the note taped to the breadbox. Maybe he'd strip and shower, which was what he did when he needed to think. Maybe he'd cruise over to the Stardust for some quick cool ones, a medium rare and sympathy. But by the time we crossed the border into Canada, and were given the welcome grandparents reserve for the black sheep of the flock, Dad would have called. She said I didn't have to fret over my baseball mitt and national park pennants, or View Master, or the orange row of Tom Swifts, or the Hardy Boys' blue spines in the bookcase, because we'd be back with Dad before I could say "Jack Robinson."

The country changed before my very eyes. The road in the mountains was slick and black, and when the bus slowed for hairpins, I looked down into the damp Northwest, at tops of trees so green they were grey. I watched my life, what was bright and hot and loud, turn into this cold, quiet, new land.

Mum wouldn't eat the devilled egg sandwiches, or cheddar cheese and crackers, she'd packed for the trip. She swallowed two Bayers with water at every stop. She kept apologizing for taking me away in the school year and remembered some sweet times she'd had with Dad. We had just passed Portland when she asked me if I'd met Susan and I said I had.

"Well?" Mum said.

"Well, what?"

"Well, what's the little golddigger like? How old is she?"

"I don't know. Twenty. Maybe that." I'd thought a lot about the night at the boarding-house. I had tried to understand why Dad had picked red-eyed Susan over Isobel, or

Nina. He had been eyeing Isobel's legs, and I'd felt embarrassed when Nina talked about toe-touches in her Texan twang, had imagined her bending over in snug shorts. Susan had been wearing a dress and crumpling a Kleenex in her fist. I couldn't explain why that girl to my mother; I just didn't know.

"Well, did you talk to her?"

"No."

Mum reached into her purse and pulled out Norman Vincent Peale's guide to positive thinking. She'd borrowed it from the library. "I think your father's told you not to talk to me about her."

"No," I said. "He doesn't know I know."

Mum opened the book and started reading. I was tired of studying the other passengers. I was tired of their necks, and hair-dos, and profiles. I was tired of staring out the window at thousands of identical evergreens floating in a pea soup fog. Mum turned a few pages and then said, "Just tell me what colour is her hair."

"Blond."

"Long?" she whispered

"Short," I said.

My grandfather met us at the Greyhound bus station in downtown New Westminster. He was wearing paint clothes and a splattered cap. He gave me my first Canadian chocolate bar, an O! Henry, and asked "Have you seen the Pacific? It's the biggest ocean in the world." When I told him I hadn't seen it close up, he wanted to take us directly there. Mum said there would be other days.

He drove us back to the house where my mother had grown up and Mum pointed, "That's the way I walked to school. There's the house I took music theory." When I ran up the steps to hug Gramma, she said I was the spitting image of my father. She'd baked a pineappple upside-down cake. I leaned against the pantry wall and got yellow paint all over my jacket.

He never telephoned. After a while, my grandparents' questions stopped and a prickly silence prevailed. I started school at Mum's old elementary and learned provinces and premiers instead of governors and states. I got used to the Pacific, to beavers and queens on nickels. On Friday nights I speed-skated at the ice rink and tripped girls for fun. Mum played organ and observed a two-drink maximum.

The divorce was begun in a few months, and finalized after a year, and then Mum married Richard Allen and moved us into his house. He owned a grandfather clock and a crank phonograph. He was older than her, and she liked that; she was 40. And she wed him because he struck her as different from Dad: instead of flamboyant, unfaithful, put off until tomorrow, Richard was dull, true, do it now and owned his own small plumbing business.

He'd never been a husband or father before. He handed me a fist of his business cards to palm off on my schoolmates, which he hoped worked their way home to parents damning leaking pipes, and he lent me a plumber's snake for Careers Week. He didn't take a shine to me though. He sat me down for a man-to-man talk and said he'd wear the pants in this particular family. He also said that Mum glimpsed my father in my face, especially when I smiled, and to be mindful of that fact.

One dismal afternoon, Mum took me out for hot chocolate at the Aristocratic and told me she was going to have a baby. "The birds and bees," she said. "Your father told you, eh?"

"Sure," I lied. It had occurred to me that my father

hadn't been paternal at all; he hadn't kept caring for my lonely mother; he hadn't fought for my custody, or called me, or sent my books and toys, and now here was something else left undone.

"Good." Mum opened her compact and dusted off the little round mirror with a fingertip.

Of course, I knew where the baby had come from. I remembered a morning when I'd felt my father's hand cold on my arm. I remembered a morning when atoms had split above the desert dust and the Earth had not since spun true.

# The Harbour

**Patricia Seaman**

And then, I wanted to give her something, badly. I took off my bracelet and held it out for her but she ignored me. Here, I said, this is for you. She wouldn't take it. You could see she thought things were beginning to happen that she didn't like. She was the kind of girl you recognize, you think you remember her from somewhere, but that's impossible. You want her to remember you. You try being especially deferential to her. It only makes her impatient. She looks around for the waiter. She'll do anything to avoid you.

Later, you find yourself thinking of her, of how mad she was. How strange it must have been for her. How maddening. How she probably won't go downtown anymore. Because of you.

She was in her early twenties, a girl with long, blonde hair, and long arms, tanned. She had clear, blue eyes. She was pretty and spoiled. She gave herself away immediately. I was sad for her. If she had known she wouldn't have cared. I was nothing to her, less than nothing. Sitting next to her I looked my age. I looked as tired as I was and as hungover.

I was wearing a faded, yellow dress. It was sticking to me from the sweat along my ribs. The dress was loose, sleeveless, plain. I wasn't wearing a belt. My only jewellery was the silver bracelet. He mentioned how tired I looked. I was pleased with myself for being that tired, that is, for having the stamina to get that tired. And for looking it. I thought I looked more interesting than their young girlfriend. She was galled at having to share her table with me. With me, to her, an old woman. For my part, I was enjoying myself. He explained her to me. This is a girl we went to high school with, he said, nothing more. She didn't like that either.

I was drinking a little bottle of mineral water. It was difficult for me to pay attention to anything. I hadn't slept in two nights. When I spoke to her she didn't answer me, she pretended not to have heard. She looked at me as if I were a crazy woman, some sort of bag lady. As if I might go out of control at any moment. As if I were uncontrollable. She addressed all her comments to him. She was mainly interested in him. However, what she said provoked an argument. He disagreed with her. He told her that she didn't know what she was talking about. She tried again. You don't know what you're talking about, he said.

He asked me if I had eaten anything. I lied to him and

said that I had. I said, I better stop drinking like this or one morning I'm going to wake up dead. This was the wrong thing to say. He didn't think it was funny. It upset him. He took it like a bad omen, or maybe he thought I was making some vague threat, which I wasn't. I hadn't meant to sound so serious. I was just sick.

There is this certain sickness that comes over you. It is when after a fitful hour of nightmares you open your eyes and feel your entire skin burning with alcohol as if someone had poured a bottle of scotch over you and set you alight. You feel like a monk. It hurts. It doesn't go away. You want to cry but you are dehydrated so you haven't got any tears, not one to spare. You want to cry out, no-one would hear you, worse, someone would hear you. At first, even drinking a glass of water makes you want to vomit. Your heart is pounding and you are sure that this time you are going to die. You are alone. Out of a pure horror of death you make it to the bathroom to get a glass of water from the faucet. It tastes like garbage; worse. You don't vomit. You resolve to live in the mountains when this is all over. You spend all day lying on the bed, not asleep. You know you are responsible for this but you'll blame anything, bad luck, or capitalism, or pesticides, or him. Finally, your skin stops burning. Still, it is so hot. You're wasting your time. Eventually you manage to shower and put on a dress because you want to see him even under the worst circumstances. You have to do it. You look like shit. You look your age. Older. You hope that at least you don't smell like a dirty old drunk. He is there, but just as you suspected, it is under the worst circumstances. Actually, it's worse than you imagined. There isn't a chance for you to be alone with him. Or, he is waiting for you in another room but you can't find him. He comes back. You are still waiting with her, still smiling at her, still drinking from a bottle of water. She won't speak to you. It's obvious why you are there. Or so you think.

And so, you say what you are thinking of. And sometimes you won't talk about anything else but that, at least you don't want to. And you get so annoyed with him because he keeps changing the subject. You think of just yelling at him but then you remember not to at the last second. So instead you say, go jump in the lake. He pretends everything is normal.

As soon as he invited me to sit with them it became strange. Conversation was strained. There was no conversation. I remembered that one night, very late, he had called me. He talked to me about God. I hadn't taken him seriously. That made him worry about my soul. I told him, my soul is none of your business. There was another explanation. He wasn't listening. Later he said he had been drunk.

His friend, who I had slept with, was there. His friend didn't speak to me or look at me. Actually, I had forgotten that I had slept with him. I only slept with him because it was what he wanted. I had no opinion about it myself. That is, at the time. I hadn't been paying any attention to him or to what was happening. He resents me now. Every time I see him he treats me coldly, even rudely. It always surprises me. I keep thinking he is a friend of mine. I keep forgetting that I slept with him. He doesn't contribute anything to the conversation other than a look of contempt. He doesn't even say anything to the girl. He wants to punish us all indiscriminately.

The friend leaves everything up to him. He pretends not to notice silence. The girl expects him to show her homage. She makes demands on him. This is her right. Her God-given right. She thinks nothing changes. She thinks she will never be alone. It's not what she has planned. His careless-ness of her is making her angry. She presses him. She hasn't learned to be with other women yet. She ignores me. She wants his undivided attention.

That's not what I want from him. What I want is to have him put his hands on me. Under my clothes. I'm wearing nothing under my dress, it's too hot, I say to myself.

All he can say to me are the most mundane things. He can't say anything else. He asks me if I have eaten. He tells me I have to stop drinking. He tells me he's tired, says he hasn't slept. Says that in a few more hours he will be a wreck. I don't ask him why. I ask him what his plans are for later. He doesn't answer my question. He is not himself. He feels sorry for me. Or else, he loves me. It's beginning to make him sick. He feels sorry for himself. He's so young. This is the first time love has made him sick.

I see one of my old lovers, he is standing at the bar with a woman I don't know. I slowly walk toward him. He looks at me, he looks pale. He would like to run away but I'm block-ing the door. Before I say anything, even before I say hello, he blames himself. We have a short, quiet argument. At the end of it I tell him to hold me, which he does. I walk back to my little party and sit beside him; if he saw any of that he doesn't let on.

Anything could happen to me like that. Like, a little girl's anger. Inexplicable. It's a mystery. Of course, I don't waste my time asking about it. Sometimes I discover it by accident. Or, by mistake, or through carelessness. For her, it must have been different, her demands, especially her demands on him, must have ensured if not exactly routine, at least a comforting predictability.

Another of my old lovers comes in the door and I make a point of speaking to him. But he's had enough of this display and gets up to walk away. He touches my arm roughly, a slap, and says they are going into the other room. I go with them, following a way behind her. I want him to know that I have an illimitable history even though it's not what I'm interested in at the moment. Nostalgia is boring. If I could I would like to make him jealous only because it would make it that much more difficult for him not to think about me. Already I know what he's going to think, there's no avoiding it. It looks bad for me.

We are like two invalids. I no longer have any will one way or the other. We have nothing to say to each other but the most essential things, did you eat, it's so hot, have you slept, are you all right. Is everything all right. Are you all right. As the city gets hotter the languor increases. Everybody is talking about the holes in the ozone. There are incredible recriminations. I am perspiring. My thighs are damp, my dress is clinging to my legs. I try to make him look at me by saying, it's so hot, and putting my hand on my wet belly. By a supreme act of will. He won't look at me.

I don't understand this about her, why she's hating me with such ardour. But I can't think straight and then I'm looking out the window, something has caught my eye, a woman in a green hat, and I've forgotten about her and her temper. I'm not looking at her so she can't make a scene. Everything I do makes it worse between us. Mostly, what she hates is that I'm drinking from a bottle of water.

The bar is airless. The cigarette smoke sticks in the back of everyone's throat. There is a loud din but when I look at people I see that hardly anyone is talking, except a few people who are shouting orders at the bartender, who moves as if he is in a vacuum. I notice that I am bored. It becomes obvious to me that this time I will live. I leave the bar without saying anything. It would have been impossible with him. We have nothing more to say to each other. He has already become unsympathetic. He blames me. So what. It's not true. I walk out the door. Outside I run into an old friend. She kisses me lightly on the lips. The streets are crowded with people looking for a place to escape the heat. All they want is to sit down. To look at people. To find an imaginary breath of air. To have a tall drink with ice, not necessarily to drink it, but just to look at. All the cafés are full, people who have found seats are not moving. They have been there since late afternoon, will not go home to their rooms until everything closes, until there is nowhere else to go.

I go into a small store and buy another bottle of water. The man behind the counter holds the bottle against his body with his arm that ends at the elbow and opens it with his one hand. Thank you, I say.

My sister and I are with some others in the dream, we are hiking in the mountains. It is dangerous, or else we aren't concerned if there is danger. We have to cross a narrow ledge to reach the path, it continues. Using both hands we dig our fingers into the holds we find in the rock, scree slides down the mountain. One at a time. As always, I live in some kind of a warehouse. There is an indeterminate light source, or else, early morning. The only furniture is an old-fashioned bed like a rich person's bed, white linen. And a wooden writing table. The room is hung with white gauze curtains. The curtains move, is there a window. I push aside the curtains to walk through the room. I am wearing a white gauze gown or vestment. My sister and I meet at the foot of the mountain on the grassy path. There are storm clouds and it's a dark morning. We don't say anything to each other or we say one thing to each other. We walk up the path. It has all been prearranged. She climbs ahead of me. I hold aside the curtains, my gown in the indeterminate wind. I take the end of the gauze, put it on the table and write on it. What I say is, he was subjugated by power and so he took power into himself. I'm talking about my brother.

There is a cement wall that separates me from the traffic. As I'm walking across the bridge I'm looking over the other wall at the train tracks. The train yard goes along the shore as far as the horizon. The tracks, ten or twelve wide in some parts, make an interesting pattern when seen from the bridge. There is an old brick station house with broken windows as well as machinery and garbage piles in the yard. I have to get across the expressway to get to the harbour.

A woman is sitting on a bench facing the lake. She has stretched her legs out in front of her. She has taken off her shoes and is wiggling her toes in the grass. She is listening to the weather report on an old transistor radio. There is an almost perceptible almost cool breeze off the lake. However, there is a bad smell. If the damn mayor wants to clean up the damn city so bloody bad why doesn't he start with the goddamn lake, she says. I sit down beside her on the bench. That's a good question.

# The Duel in Cluny Park

**Timothy Findley**

The duel in Cluny Park took place just after dawn on a Sunday morning—16 December, in 1979. That was the day when it also snowed for eighteen hours, nonstop. Two shots were fired—and only two, in spite of the fact that various people later were to claim that three or four had been heard. These phantom shots were more than likely echoes bouncing off the fieldstone walls that separated the park from various private gardens rising up behind the houses on Cluny Drive and Crescent Road.

Because of its shape, its size and its situation, Cluny Park was sometimes called the Pocket. Someone would ring you up on a clear, bright day and say, "We're going to have a picnic down in the Pocket." Then out would come the Embros hampers stuffed with pâté and salads and potted shrimp from David Wood and breads and brioche from Patachou and tall, cool bottles of frosted Riesling and sparkling cider from the Liquor Board. Coloured blankets and tablecloths would be spread out wide on the ground and, if anyone looked down from the houses through the trees, the picnickers would be seen in their summer whites and wide-brimmed hats, raising their glasses to toast the sun. A lot of people miss that, now.

The park itself was little more than a bit of grass enclosed in a small ravine, the sides of which were steep enough in places to give the impression of peril. Standing, for instance, in Andrew and Hazel Cournoyer's grove of Japanese maples, you had the distinct sensation that one false step would send you tumbling all the way to the bottom. This, while not exactly reassuring, at least provided a view that was picturesque in a postcard sort of way. A postcard showing Edwardian revellers in one of those charming bubcolic settings to have passed forever, along with England.

To those who lived on its verges, Cluny Park was a private, pleasant and well-kept secret. Pleasant, at least, until that Sunday morning in December of 1979 when Mary Jane Powell and Bobby Finster fought their duel there and one of them was killed.

Andrew and Hazel Cournoyer were giving a black and white party to celebrate their tenth anniversary. *The anniversary,* as Hazel said in her telephoned invitations, *where everyone gives you something made of tin....*

Bobby and Margot Finster were taking along a pair of tin snips—or shears (they had argued about the name)—in the hopes that everyone else would be giving something funny like old tin cans and the snips would come in handy. "We can cut out rows of tin dolls," Bobby said. Margot had wrapped the shears up in tinfoil, tied with a large black bow.

"Why do I keep on thinking 15 December is a date in history?" Margot said as she and Bobby were driving down through the twilight to Cluny Drive. It was Saturday night.

Bobby said: "Because it is. Fifteen December was your mother's birthday."

He smiled—and Margot smiled back.

"My mother isn't *history*," she said.

"She is now," said Bobby. "Dead four years and mourned every minute of her absence."

"Do you mean that?"

"Sure I do. Your mother was terrific. She was something to celebrate. Not many mothers are."

"You make me nervous, talking like that."

"Good heavens, why?"

"You're implying that, as mothers go, I may not be worth celebrating...."

Margot turned away and looked out the window of the car—their very first Jaguar. Bobby looked over and took his hand from the wheel just long enough to give Margot's hair a brush with the backs of his fingers.

"You've got to forget it, M," he said. "You are one hell of a mother. Our kids adore you—and their adoration is real."

"I know that. But..." Margot looked down in her lap and found her evening bag. Silver—to go with her silver dress. She got out a packet of DuMauriers and lighted one.

"But nothing." Bobby resettled his arm against his side, the fingers of his right hand grazing the wheel above his crotch. He was horny tonight. He could almost feel the heat rising up from where he sat. Something more than Margot—or the thought of Margot—was doing it; something about the red leather seats, the smells inside the car, including Margot's perfume; something about the boxer shorts he was wearing, the way they let his penis out through their open fly so it touched the wool of his trousers; the always sensuous irritation of evening clothes.

"You've got to stop thinking about it, M," (was he talking to himself or to her?) "now and forever—put it in the past. It's done. It was not your fault. Let's talk about, think about something else. Okay?"

"Okay." She smiled. He was right. It hadn't been her fault. But it was all so wrong—so pointless; she would never get over that. The deaths of all children are pointless and wrong. Nothing anyone could say would ever give them credence or rightness.

They were driving down to Rosedale from Warren Road in Forest Hill and had reached the corner of St. Clair and Yonge. Everywhere around them, the coloured lights in all the windows of all the shops and restaurants were proclaiming A MERRY CHRISTMAS AND A HAPPY NEW YEAR! Margot tried not to read them. The coloured lights in themselves were not problematical—but the message, the goddamned message....

The goddamned message was like a goad. It was almost evil, somehow, as if every shop and restaurant owner and every window decorator in Toronto was out to taunt her with their goddamned messages of love, good cheer and hope.

If only it hadn't happened at Christmastime....

*She's dead. Sara Finster. Dead.*

*Climbed up over the kitchen sink to turn on the light—and had one hand on a running tap—just like that—aged five.*

*Five and would now have been seven.*

Bobby shifted gear and looked at Margot again and said, "Stop that right now, or we're going home."

He meant it. He was angry.

"Yes, yes," said Margot. "I've stopped. I really have..." She got out some Kleenex and blew her nose. "It was just those bloody words done up in lights in all those windows."

They drove in silence until they came to Inglewood Drive, where Bobby Finster turned the Jaguar toward the Mt. Pleasant cutoff, heading south.

Just past the lip of the hill Margot said, "There's a dead dog lying in the road back there."

"I know," said Bobby. "I saw it."

He kept on going.

"Why did they leave it lying there in the middle of the road like that? Why can't they move it over to the curb, at least?"

Bobby said nothing.

Then he said: "All right. You win," and he threw the car into reverse, spinning it backwards up the hill through all the downward spinning others.

Margot, alarmed, was afraid her remark about the dog being left on the road was going to drive them home—as if, somehow, the dog on the road and the forbidden subject of Sara's death were inextricably connected.

"I only meant...," she began.

"Be quiet," said Bobby.

They had reached the place where the dog was lying, caught in the streaming lights of the passing cars. It had snowed about an hour before, and the road was bright and wet and dangerous.

"Move him," said Bobby, not unkindly, once he had drawn the Jaguar into the curb and shut off the motor. "I'll wait here."

Margot turned to him and beamed.

"Thank you," she said. "I knew I had married a god of mercy! I'll be as fast as I can."

The traffic was intermittent, and as Margot left the car, the only thing approaching was one of those gigantic tractor-trailers with its pup in tow. It was shifting gears with a lot of violent wrenching and farting noises down at the bottom of the hill. Margot removed her cashmere shawl with its glass and silver passementerie and threw it back inside the car. Her shoes would be problematical because of their heels—but she dare not remove them for fear her stockings would be torn.

"You won't need your handbag, M," said Bobby, and Margot threw that back into the car as well. She left the door open—an open door was a means of escape—and it also meant: *I'm coming back.*

She now had to wait for three cars to pass, each one of them veering at a different speed around the dog in its path—one of them honking loudly, angrily: *how dare this bloody dog lie down and die in front of my Volvo station-wagon!*

Bobby was watching the tractor-trailer lumbering up by the opposite curb, its driver, still not seeing Margot, staring blankly through his windshield muttering something, maybe the words of a song....

Margot strode out to where the dog was lying. She was relatively confident that she would not be hit in her silver dress. It acted as a great reflector.

Watching her, Bobby realized that here was one of the

mysteries of Margot; her integrity showed itself in simple, almost childish ways: that dogs who had died should not be left like garbage on the road. And...

The dog wagged its tail.

It was alive.

Margot was bending over it—stupefied. The dog looked back into her face and thumped its tail against the road three times.

Margot looked across at Bobby, waved her arm and Bobby waved back. *Get off the goddamned road, Margot.*

Two more cars went by, not even pausing. The tractor-trailer was disappearing up toward St. Clair.

Margot reached down under the dog and hauled it up against her waist. Its body was cold and stiff and matted with bits of ice. It was a terrier, perhaps, though that was hard to tell; either an Irish terrier or a slightly mongrelized Airedale. It cried out once when she lifted it. Why was it so heavy, when it seemed so small? She tried to hold it firmly so it wouldn't bend, in case its back was broken, or its ribs. But, just as she got it over to the curb, its head lolled down and the weight became untenable. Blood spilled out of its mouth. It died.

*Dear dog,* she thought. *I'm sorry.*

Bobby leaned over and called through the open door. "Okay?"

"It's dead," said Margot—and laid it out on the ground.

"All right," said Bobby. And then he said: "Come on back, M. Get into the car. You've done your duty. We have to go."

*We have to go. We have to go,* said Margot, in her mind, addressing the lifeless dog at her feet. *We have to go. To a goddamn party. I'm sorry. Your people will find you here when they come out looking, tomorrow.*

She started back to the car, but before she got inside she turned around and said, "Goodbye."

Sitting, warm again, next to Bobby as he turned the key and they started south, Margot closed her eyes. *He knew someone cared,* she thought. *Before he died, the dog knew someone cared.*

"Are you all right?"

Margot said nothing. She wondered what Bobby could possibly mean.

Coming into the dip before the rise to Roxborough Drive, they saw another dog, this one alive. It was loping along beside the road, looking as if it knew where it was going.

*There,* thought Bobby. *That'll cheer her up.* "Looks pretty happy to me," he said.

*Yes,* Margot thought, *which is always when something dreadful happens....*She did not say this out loud. Instead, she speculated about the guest list for the Cournoyers' party.

"The Powells are going to be there, sure as fate," she said, making sure she was smiling when she said it. "They're everywhere you go these days."

"That's because Mary Jane is waiting to make his move. He doesn't dare give up a single opportunity. He even goes and sits in the sauna bath at the B and R—and waits. He hangs around the urinals at the Toronto Club...."

"You're kidding!"

"Yes. I'm kidding. Not about the sauna—that much is true. Mary Jane knows that, one day, Brian Gossage and Gordon Perry are going to have to walk in there and he'll be waiting. But not by the urinals, no."

"Why do they call him *Mary Jane?* I've never understood that," said Margot.

"I don't think I do, either. His initials, though, are M.J. Stands for *something* Jackman. The M, I don't know."

"I wondered if it had to do with marijuana."

"Marijuana?"

"Don't you remember? They used to call marijuana *Mary Jane.* I wondered if that was why."

"Somehow, I doubt it," said Bobby. "If Mary Jane Powell is getting off on drugs, it wouldn't be marijuana."

"You mean cocaine?"

"Oh, no. Much stronger than that, I think."

"Heroin? Heavens!"

"No. Not heroin, either. *Money.*"

Bobby laughed.

"Ah, yes." Margot settled back and pulled her cashmere closer round her shoulders. *That* drug."

"The best we have," said Bobby, smiling.

Margot smiled back. "Yeah," she said. "I kinda get off on money, myself."

They were now on Crescent Road, where several of the houses sported coloured lights around their doors and strings of blue and white bulbs in the spruce and cedar trees or winking on and off along the bare, wet arms of magnolias.

"I always feel safe in here," said Margot—meaning Rosedale.

Bobby didn't answer. He was watching a group of teenage carol singers moving along the sidewalk, coming in their direction. It was good, he thought, to see them there—the carrying on of old traditions was always a hopeful sign....

"Look at their faces," said Margot. Her voice had gone white. She drew back further into the Jaguar, thinking—she did not know why—*I mustn't let them see me.*

Bobby looked. He still couldn't make out what had alarmed her.

"Put on your glasses!" said Margot, hoarse and whispering. "Look."

Bobby put on his glasses—steel-rimmed and cold. And while he did this, the Jaguar almost glided to a stop.

Their faces....

Holy shit.

The faces of the carol singers were covered with smooth brown leather masks. Helmets were fitted over their heads like skin—black leather helmets—brown leather faces. All that could be seen that was human were the whites of eyes and the shapes of mouths and nostrils, the mouths exhaling visible, pale grey bursts of breath.

The Jaguar was idling, it seemed, of its own accord.

One of the singers stepped off the sidewalk onto the street and ran a leather hand along the side of the car.

Bobby flicked the door locks. *Click.* It sounded like a small explosion. The other singers were gathering, now, around the car, some of them pressing their faces close against the window glass.

"Don't say anything," Bobby muttered. "Don't say anything."

They sat completely still—the way they might have sat through the final seconds in a theatre before the curtain rose. Margot wanted to close her eyes but couldn't.

"*God rest ye merry, gentlemen,*" the singers sang. "*Let nothing you dismay.*"

They sang it almost as a lullaby might have been sung, while they rocked the car gently side to side. And then they drew away—they even waved—and were gone.

Margot felt the car regain its power and saw the trees beside her move.

Bobby picked up speed, said nothing and turned the corner onto Cluny Drive.

They were there. Number 36.

Margot sat still. There was blood on her silver dress.

Bobby got out and walked around the car. He was carrying the snips done up in foil and all the long black ribbons were hanging down towards the snow.

He opened the door.

"Come on," he said. "We're going inside to celebrate."

The first thing Margot Finster heard when she reached the hall was her father's voice. This was not something she had expected, and she turned to Bobby with a look that was half alarm and half chagrin. Before she could speak, however, Hazel Cournoyer was leaning in toward her, smelling of too much Opium and turning her red-red cheeks this way and that while making kiss-kiss noises and saying, "We think it's so wonderful you could come...." As if some circumstance unknown to Margot might have precluded her arrival.

"I need to go upstairs," she said. "Upstairs or into the kitchen. I've a stain on my dress and...."

"Not in the kitchen!" said Hazel, over-reacting, as always, to everything. "The kitchen is just a mass of surprises! I wouldn't have you discover them for all the world, not till we're all at table together. Come upstairs. I'll help you..."

They started cross the hallway, which was wide and marbled and tricky to negotiate because of all the mirrors. Andrew and Hazel went through phases of manic collecting and Japanese lacquer had given way the previous summer to rococo mirrors.

"I thought I heard my father's voice," said Margot, attempting nonchalance. "I love your dress. I hadn't expected him to be here. Is something going on besides your anniversary?"

"No, of course not," said Hazel. "Yours is nice, too. It's just that Andrew wanted to spread the generations a little wider than usual. Says he gets sick of the same old healthy faces.... They make him feel inferior. We haven't been to Peebee once this season."

"Well, it's a little early, yet," said Margot. "No-one you'd really want to see arrives in Peebee till after New Year's, anyway."

They were almost halfway up the stairs and Margot, preparing to negotiate the landing, turned and gazed back at the scene below them: Bobby adjusting his tie in one of the mirrors; Andrew Cournoyer crossing the black and white marble with Cybil Torrance and Peter Bongard, all of them laughing, Cybil tall in a long white dress, pale as an elegant Amazon. Alan Northey, nervous in a doorway, was fingering a glass of Perrier and listening to John Dai Bowen explain—for the hundredth time, no doubt—why Fabiana Holbach was God's best gift to fashion photography, in spite of the fact she hated having her picture taken....

These were all people of Margot's generation—as Hazel was: the crop of the early fifties and mid-to-late forties— none of them older than thirty-five—all of them bound together by virtue of their schools and money and mutual inclinations to cluster at the foot of Bay Street, where their fathers' names were framed in mahogany and set in brass.

*Alexander Peyton Wood.*

There he was, in his dreadful brocade jacket, worn every Christmas and New Year's, his Chinese velvet pumps and his scarlet complexion—the tallest man and the thinnest in the world—with the reediest, most off-putting voice. Her father—looking up at her.

44

Margot turned away and continued to climb beyond the landing, out of sight.

Hazel, climbing beside her and reaching down to lift the silver folds of Margot's dress, was saying: "What on earth is this? It looks like blood."

"It is," said Margot. She did not explain.

Everyone had done as they were told and across the hall from the sitting-room where most of the guests had gathered before the fire, a table had been prepared to receive the gifts of tin. This was in the library, where the books stood up in unread rows that reached the ceiling. Guests, on occasion, perused the titles—but that was the extent of their attraction. The room was normally given over to games of trivia and bridge and, very often, to games of chance where the stakes were high and money changed hands without a thought about where it was going.

*Money has no loyalties,* Andrew Cournoyer had said, in one of his brighter moments. *You have to tie it down.* He was not, however, much in the habit of losing.

Andrew played his cards and dice with skill and the kind of concentration only professionals bring to games. He was dangerous in there, in the so-called library, whereas, beyond its walls, he was perceived only as Hazel's boyish husband—charming, but unassuming. People were always saying of him, *what does Andrew do?* because he was not the sort of man who could be identified by means of what he did. Whatever he did, he did as a dabbler. Andrew was never seen downtown except as a guest at other people's clubs. Whatever he did, it left no mark on him except the marks of ingratiation and availability: nervous eyes and a willing mouth. All of this changed when he stood inside the walls of number 36 Cluny Drive, inviting you in amongst the books for a game of seven-card stud or three-card monte.

Now, however, the library had been commandeered for the display of anniversary tin, which covered the length and depth of one whole table, twelve feet long. A tin cage with tin birds sitting amongst tin flowers sat in the middle of the table, surrounded by tin candlesticks, tin motorcars, tin cows and horses and a pear tree made of tin with boxes numbered from one to twelve beside it, each box containing one new day of Christmas, starting with a partridge made of tin and, buried at the bottom, twelve tin drummers drumming. Bobby and and Margot Finster's snipshears had been unpacked and added to this loot—ribbons, tinfoil and all.

"Thank God this wasn't their fiftieth anniversary," said Conrad Fastbinder, standing in the doorway looking in with grim amusement. "I'd hate to think what twelve gold days of Christmas might have cost."

Margot Finster and Claire Bongard were standing by the fire enjoying, as always, one another's company. In their final year together at Branksome Hall, Claire had been head girl and Margot had been her confidante. Claire had always been immensely popular—nervously vital, talented, unpredictable. Now, in her adult life, the innocence of her appeal had failed to hold its own in the face of her increased demand that she be loved. A kind of chaos had come into her eyes. Even as she stood with you, she abandoned you and wandered off—afraid—into her own private world. Her left hand very often rose up under her chin where her fingers played with a chain that wasn't there.

She had married Peter Bongard at the age of seventeen. Rumour had it now that the Bongards were going their separate ways. At the Cournoyers' party, Peter had arrived with Cybil Torrance and Claire had arrived with someone she introduced to Margot Finster only as "a man called Orenstein."

"This is a man called Orenstein," she'd said, and had sent him off to talk to Alan Northey.

Now, Claire was saying, "Did you ever think, then—when we were girls—we would have to pay for our sins?"

Margot laughed. "No," she said. "Sins? What sins?" Claire leaned against the mantelpiece and threw her cigarette into the flames. "*Sins.* You know. Just being who we are."

Margot felt cold in spite of the fire. "I don't understand what you mean," she said. Claire turned partway around and nodded at the room with its clusters of chatting guests and its ebullient hosts. "I mean that," said Claire. "Those people. Them and us—and who we are."

"I never think about who we are at all," said Margot, smiling at Bobby, who stood about ten feet away talking to John Dai Bowen and Fabiana Holbach. "I like who we are and I don't know what you mean by *sin.*"

Claire blinked. She looked confused. Perhaps she had been inside her private world.

"You don't?" she said.

"No. I don't," said Margot, still smiling. "You're not a sinner, Claire. You've just had rotten luck, that's all."

As soon as she'd said this, Margot wavered. She had seen her father watching her from across the room and something inside her fell to one side. A door came open inside and she had a view of what Claire meant—but only for an instant. The words *my father, my father* occurred to her. *Bang!* And the door slammed shut.

Claire said, "I want a drink."

"Me, too," said Margot.

But just as they began to make their way cross the room toward the barman, the doorbell rang.

Margot had been quite right.

It was Mary Jane Powell and a party of six.

"See who Mary Jane has with him," said Claire.

"Your sister-in-law," said Margot.

"Susan?"

"Yes."

"Well, well," said Claire. "The son of a bitch deserves the bitch."

Margot winced. Susan Bongard was someone she rather liked.

"On the other hand," said Claire, "the bitch does not deserve the son of a bitch. No-one deserves the son of a bitch. He's a cannibal."

"Yes," said Magot. "With that, I agree."

But Margot was not concerned about Mary Jane Powell and Susan Bongard. She was concerned about the others who had come in with them. Brian Gossage and Gordon Perry. Again, she had been right. This was not a simple cele-bration of the Cournoyers' tenth anniversary. This was something else entirely.

They ate at two round tables for ten. Margot and Bobby were separated and Margot began to panic. It was not the fact of their separation that bothered her so much as the fact that Andrew's table, where Bobby was seated, was pre-dominantly occupied by the group that had arrived with Mary Jane Powell and his brother, Tom. Apparently, Mary Jane Powell had sweated long enough in the B and R sauna to be there when Gossage and Perry at last arrived.

The seating arrangements had not been meant to work

out this way, and all through the soup Hazel Cournoyer kept apologizing. "I am so dreadfully distressed," she said at least three times. "I cannot abide the thought of a table made up entirely—well, almost entirely—of men. It means there will not be a single word of civilized conversation."

"I absolutely agree with you," said Tina Perry, who was small and tough and spent her life pursuing golf and tennis balls. She was wearing black, which showed off her tan and her hair, dyed honey blond. She was sitting next to Margot, whom she disliked intensely because she thought that Margot was responsible for Gordon Perry's infatuation with Bobby Finster. *Margot Finster is the kind of woman,* Tina Perry had once told Hazel Cournoyer, *who gets behind her husband and pushes him into places he does not belong.* Of course, there was not a word of truth in this, but there was nothing Margot could do but live with Tina's opinion. Gordon Perry, after all, was Bobby's mentor in the corporate world. The older man's affection for his protégé was almost that of a father for a son—and Bobby had neither objected to their relationship nor rejected the advancements it had brought him. *I would do anything for Gordon Perry,* Bobby had once declared in Margot's presence.

Margot had cringed at this enthusiasm—knowing as she did that Gordon Perry's affections could be dangerous. Long ago, he had made a leap in loyalties that had brought his best friend close to ruin, but nothing had ever been proved, nor could it be, because the leap had been made behind closed doors. This had been when Gordon Perry established his credentials with Alex Peyton Wood, back in the time when Margot was still a child and could only guess at the devastation caused when what her mother had called "the knives" came out. The man who was nearly ruined had been her mother's brother—her beloved Uncle Terry, long since dead—and the ruin was completed when her mother died.

Bobby Finster had never believed this story. Gordon Perry was incapable, in Bobby's eyes, of anything that smelled of blood. Everyone knew that Uncle Terry's business failures had been brought about by his innate lack of business sense. *He was a charming, arrogant fool,* the story went, as Bobby told it, *who couldn't read the writing on the wall....*

Now, as the shrimps in a ginger sauce were being served, Margot prayed those words would not, one day, be said about Bobby—who, himself, was an "arrogant fool" where Gordon Perry was concerned. Not because Bobby could not, but because he would not read the writing on the walls—made every day more evident by Gordon Perry's restless shifting in Mary Jane Powell's direction.

Claire, who seemed increasingly ill at ease, had excused herself before the shrimp arrived and had gone outside to "get some fresh air and smoke a cigarette." The man called Orenstein, who was sitting next to Margot, turned to her and said, "You see that man over there—the one they call Mary Jane?"

Margot nodded, dreading what might be coming— some paean of manly praise, no doubt, a round of applause for the joys of climbing in Mary Jane's company up the ladder of success, larded with phrases like "golden boy" and "wunderkind"....

"I nearly killed him once," said Orenstein.

"You did?" said Margot—delighted and trying not to show it.

"Yes," said the man called Orenstein, reaching out sadly for his glass of wine. "He fucked my wife at a party back in 1975."

"At a party," said Margot.

"Yes, ma'am. A party. In Montreal."

Orenstein took a long, slow pull at his wine and rolled the stem of the glass between his fingers.

Margot waited. But that was apparently all the man called Orenstein had to say. It was as if, in saying that Mary Jane Powell had fucked his wife at a party in Montreal, Mister Orenstein had told her the story of his life.

And, in his way, he had.


"If anyone wants to see the seventh wonder of the world," said Claire, who had just returned from her breath of air, "you had best come now and see it before it disappears."

"What are you talking about?" said Hazel, verging on annoyance. She had just been about to call for removal of the shrimp and the serving of the grapefruit sorbet. "I don't want to say," said Claire, "because I don't want to ruin the effect. How do I get to your terrace? Down these stairs?"

She was heading for the far end of the dining-room, which faced the ravine at the back of the house.

Claire's mysterious invitation was sufficient excuse for half the guests to rise and follow her—and, once this exodus had been begun, the rest of the guests got up and made for the stairs.

"I don't know where we're going," said Cybil Torrance. "Does she really want us to go outside? I'm going to get my wrap...."

"Bring mine," said someone else.

"And mine!" said Tina Perry.

Margot had set her cashmere shawl on the back of her chair and, taking it, she also brought her glass of wine and started along the room.

On the way down the stairs, she put her free hand on

Bobby's arm and whispered, "I hope you're not in danger over there at that other table."

"Me?"

"Yes, you. The lot of you look quite sinister."

"Sinister!" Bobby was laughing.

"Yes. Like a swarm of deadly insects, my darling. What is going on?"

"A deal," said Bobby.

"Dear God, no. With *them?*"

"Not to worry. I'm not involved. But it's quite exciting."

"Sure," said Margot. "I'll bet."

During their Edwardian phase, the Cournoyers had built a conservatory leading to the terrace which led, in its turn, to the hillside garden hanging over Cluny Park.

The conservatory was filled with nonexotic, relatively hardy flowering shrubs and miniature trees and groves of bamboo shoots in pots. A pool with goldfish pulled the eye towards one side, where wicker and wrought iron garden furniture provided a resting place beneath the branches of a lemon tree.

On arrival in the conservatory, it was evident the seventh wonder of the world could not be seen from there. The doors stood open leading to the terrace.

Margot drew her shawl around her shoulders before she walked out, and took a sip of wine.

Alex Peyton Wood was waiting just inside the doors to let her pass.

"Good evening, Father."

"Margot."

"It's been a while."

"Yes."

"Do I find you well?"

"You find me as you find me," he said.

"And what does that mean?"

"Old," said Peyton Wood.

Margot went through and they said no more. On the terrace, she wanted to stand with Bobby, but he was standing, hands in pockets over near the furthest edge against the darkness with Mary Jane and Gordon Perry and Brian Gossage and Mary Jane's brother, Tom. Margot hung back and stood alone. Alex Peyton Wood went over. Everyone was looking at the sky.

"What is it? What?"

The sky was luminous back beyond the house, to the east. A colour that could only be described as smoky-orange infused the clouds of carbon compounds lying like a veil above the city. "Fire," somebody said.

"And a big one, too," someone added.

"No," said Claire. "It isn't fire. It's the seventh wonder of the world. Be patient. And be quiet...."

Everyone stood on the terrace, each one staring upward—some with napkins, others with wine glasses, some in overcoats or furs, others with upturned collars or scarves or shawls, some standing absolutely still while others swayed from foot to foot in the cold with all their breaths making shorter and shorter bursts of white as they grew impatient. "What?" "What?" "Where?"

And then it rose.

The seventh wonder of the world.

The moon.

It was red—almost as red as a blood orange is red when it is cut in half.

"Oh!"

"My!"

"Goodness!"

"Look at that…!"

Each voice was barely raised above a whisper.

"I swear you can see it moving," said Susan Bongard.

"You can. You can see it moving," said Fabiana Holbach.

"Oh, how beautiful…," said Andrew Cournoyer. "I don't believe I'm seeing this."

"And me without a camera," said John Dai Bowen.

"*The night the moon was red,*" said Claire.

"Sort of like the night they murdered Caesar," said Conrad Fastbinder.

"Good for you, Connie," said Claire. "There's always someone who brings it crashing down to earth."

"I'm cold," said Hazel.

"So am I," said Tina Perry.

"To hell with this," said Mary Jane Powell. "I'm going inside."

Mary Jane was halfway across the terrace when the singing started. It stopped him in his tracks.

*Silent night, holy night,*
*All is calm,*
*All is bright.…*

Margot shivered, thinking of the leather masks and helmets—thinking of Sara Finster, reaching out to turn on the light.

Bobby Finster turned away, perhaps because he was thinking of the leather faces, too. From the terrace, given the bare winter trees, he could see all the way to Cluny Park—spread out white and almost phosphorescent below them.

The moon rose up, immense, above the house and its light grew less and less red and more and more golden; copper; orange.

Andrew and Hazel Cournoyer and all their guests were

silent—waiting for the song to end.

*Sleep in heavenly peace,*
*Sleep in heavenly peace....*

It was done—and, lingering for one last look at the moon, they made their way inside across the stones and through the doors and under the trees and the frosted glass and up the stairs towards the remaining courses of the meal.

Alan Northey, who knew such things, was saying, as he left the terrace: "The moon should not have been that colour. Not in this season. What we have seen is truly a phenomenon."

Margot waited. Her left hand was fisted, her right hand held the wine glass close between her breasts.

Bobby came back from the edge and over the stones and stood beside her.

"Yes?" he said.

"I'm going home," said Margot.

"You can't go home. We haven't eaten yet."

"I've eaten all I can. I'm leaving."

He knew she could not by any means be made or persuaded to stay. Something had caught her and wouldn't let go.

"I'm afraid," she said. "And I wish you'd come with me."

"No, no. I can't," he said. "Impossible. But—here you take the car...." He handed her the keys and kissed her on the mouth. She tasted of wine and salt. She did not kiss back. Her eyes were open. She took his hands in her fist—with the keys between his flesh and hers.

"Will you promise to come as soon as you can?"

"I will."

"I love you."

"Yes. I love you, too."

They went upstairs.

There would come a time in later years, as Claire's own story unfolded, when those who recalled these events would say of Andrew and Hazel Cournoyer's tenth anniversary party: *that was the night before the duel in Cluny Park; the night Claire Bongard came inside and told us she had seen the moon on fire.*

Everyone knows that someone else must always be made to take responsibility for what goes wrong. And so it was that Claire and the moon were blamed for the duel in Cluny Park. The others all said, *I don't remember. I wasn't there. I didn't see. What moon...?*

Consequently, because she was the only one who truly wasn't there, the stories that Margot Finster was told about the duel in Cluny Park were made up of elements as disparate and incomplete as these:

*If the moon had not turned red....*

*If Claire had not come in and told us so....*

*If Bobby Finster had sat at Hazel's table, not at Andrew's....*

*If Mary Jane Powell had refrained from fucking Orenstein's wife....*

*If Margot had paid attention when her father said: I'm old....*

*If Margot had not gone home....*

But none of these things was the cause of the duel in Cluny Park. The cause was in the turning of a card.

Mary Jane Powell was a man both cautiously revered and hated. No-one spoke ill of him, ever, to his face.

The golden colour of his skin, the impossible blue of his eyes, the width of his mouth, the breadth of his hands and the way he stood were magnets whose power could draw you in, no matter what your age or sex. When he spoke, he leaned in close so you could feel his breath and smell his hair. His voice was seldom raised—except in moments of utter jubilation, and these were rarely come upon in a life that was lived almost entirely on the verge of imminent collapse. He so rarely failed, on the other hand, that when he spoke of these imminent dangers no-one could understand why he seemed so watchful always—always keyed and in gear—never for a moment seeming to be aware of fear.

But Mary Jane—whose given names were Mainwaring Jackman—had once encountered a wall he could neither scale nor demolish: his father. And this experience of coming up against an immovable object had left him wary forever after, certain that somewhere, sometime, another immovable object would loom in his path and he wanted to be ready for it.

Mary Jane's father, whose name was Sydney Powell, was Chairman and President of Dorchester Trust. He sat behind a polished length of barren table, showing the world he had no weapons but his will and his wits. Sitting there one day, when Mary Jane was 21 years old, Sydney Powell had rejected his son's proposal that he be his father's partner and, looking down 40 storeys over Sherbrooke Street in Montreal, he had told his son, *I wouldn't have you seen in my company. No. I will not touch you with a ten-foot pole.*

Mary Jane had been astonished. Why had his father refused him?

Because, while Sydney Powell admired and had even encouraged the killer instinct in both his sons and his daughter, he feared, from this son, the focus of that instinct.

He said, in a word, he was afraid of patricide. *I like it here, where I sit,* he told Mary Jane. *And I don't intend to share it with anyone. And especially not an assassin.*

Mary Jane often told this story, laughing as he did so. It

was one of the tales he told at business lunches. *People should know who I am,* he liked to say.

And people did.

He was 28 years old and on his way to the fourth of his millions.

The door to the library was closed. The men from Andrew's table had gone in there an hour ago and Tina Perry was raging in the living-room about the fact that Hazel had still not managed to put her foot down.

"I'm going to buy you a large pair of boots," she said. "I shall come, if I must, and give you lessons. The men must not be allowed to do this to us. It is monstrous!"

"Do what?" said Claire.

"Ensconce themselves in that room. Are you aware of what they're doing in there?"

"Well, I doubt they're having sex, Tina," said Claire.

"They are gambling away our fortunes!" Tina bellowed.

Hazel smiled. If that, indeed, was what the men were doing, then Andrew would probably do very well.

She wondered aloud if anyone would like more coffee.

"No," said Tina. "I'd like a double scotch—straight up."

Half an hour later, or thereabouts, voices were raised beyond the library door and Hazel became alarmed. It wasn't like Andrew to permit such things. Furthermore, it wasn't like their friends to do them.

"What do you think it can be about?" said Cybil Torrance. The shouting had now gone on for over five minutes.

"For all we know," said Hazel, "it could be part of the game. There are such games, you know—where people shout as part of the proceedings...."

"Prize fights, yes," said Claire.

"Do you think we should go and break it up?" said Susan Bongard. "I'm gettting more than nervous."

"No," said Hazel. "Please. Sit down."

She refused to believe that anything like an argument—let alone a fight—could happen at one of her parties. Thank God Zena Cherry hadn't been invited. She'd have had it in *The Globe and Mail* before the guests were halfway home.

*"Brian Gossage, Chairman and President of Amaken; Gordon Perry, Amaken's Executive Vice-Chairman; Robert Finster, President of Canwood and their spouses were involved in a verbal fracas the other night with Montreal's notorious gift to the business community, bad boy M.J. Powell. The fight took place at the home of Andrew Cournoyer, the noted collector, and his wife, Hazel. The cause, we are told, was...*

The door flew open at that very moment and Andrew came across the hall and into the living-room pale as the snow that had just begun to fall outside.

"What is wrong?" asked Hazel, sitting down—prepared for the worst; perhaps the loss of all they owned, considering Andrew's state.

Andrew was coming straight toward her, reaching out for the brandy decanter that sat on the table just in front of her chair.

"What is it, Andrew? What?"

Tina intervened and grabbed him by the arm.

"Tell us what has happened!"

"There is going to be a duel," said Andrew.

"A *duel?*" Claire burst out laughing.

No-one else spoke.

Claire sat down. *This isn't funny, she thought. That moon....*

59

"Will someone die?" Cybil asked.

Andrew turned around and walked away. He had arrangements to make.

Four hours later, when it was not quite 3 AM, Bobby Finster and Claire Bongard were sitting in the conservatory drinking cognac beneath the lemon tree.

Bobby had accepted Andrew's offer of a Browning .38, the only handgun kept in the house. Mary Jane Powell had sent his brother Tom to fetch the Luger he had bought from a German acquaintance in 1973. These were the weapons. Bobby Finster hadn't fired a gun in more than a dozen years.

"I wish I could understand," said Claire, "why you feel you have to do this."

"Honour."

"Honour?"

"That's right. And please don't sneer."

"I'm sorry," said Claire. "I didn't mean to sneer. I meant to laugh."

"It has to be done, whatever you think."

"Yes," said Claire. "I dare say."

She looked at him. He was such a likeable man, with his boyish hair and hazel eyes behind those crazy glasses. "Take them off," she said to him, reaching over and removing them. "You're so good-looking without them."

"A lot of good it does me," said Bobby, and he took the glasses back and settled them on his nose. "Without them, I have to stand so near the mirror to see myself, I squish my nose on the glass."

The both laughed lightly at that and then Claire took his hand and began to massage it between her own.

"I'll pay whatever losses there were," she said, "if you'd

only call this off. I'm loaded with the stuff, you know. And you could pay me back if you want to, later on. Please don't do this, Bobby. It isn't fair to Margot...."

"Margot will never know it happened," said Bobby. "Unless you tell her, of course." He smiled.

"She'll know it happened if you're killed."

"I won't be killed. There will be no killing."

Claire let go of his hand and stood up.

"I won't believe you're that naive," she said. "Are you saying you think he won't at least try to kill you?"

"I think he wouldn't dare."

Claire was silent. Then she said, "It's a pity, you know, you're not a woman."

"What the hell do you mean by that?"

"I mean that if you were a woman—and you had slept with M.J. Powell—you would know that he's a killer."

Bobby looked up from under his tousled hair at Claire.

"You've slept with him?"

"Yes."

She turned away.

Bobby ran his finger along his lip and was surprised to feel how dry it was.

"Killers have a certain rhythm, Bobby. A way of fucking that gives them away."

Bobby began to wish that Claire would stop. He did not know why, but his heart was beating somewhere in his ears and it frightened him.

He poured another drink and closed his eyes.

"I'm going to sleep," he said. "I'm going to sleep for half an hour."

Claire turned around and told him not to worry. She would sit there with him and wake him up when it was time.

Everyone had decided to stay. It seemed the wisest thing to do—since each of them would need the other's protection once the duel had been fought and the outcome was known. Everyone must tell the same story—whatever happened.

Susan and Peter Bongard—both of them lawyers, the children of lawyers—and Cybil Torrance, the daughter of one of Ontario's Supreme Court judges, sat as if in conference at one of the round white tables in the dining-room. The lights, on dimmers, had been lowered and all the reflections in the windows looked like golden optical illusions.

"What exactly happened?" said Cybil.

Peter said: "Bobby caught Mary Jane cheating. Mary Jane denied it. Bobby wouldn't accept the denial. Mary Jane challenged him to a duel."

Susan snorted—almost laughing. "It sounds like a game that kids would play. You be Clint Eastwood and I'll be Robert Redford...."

"Well," said Peter, "of course we all thought that Mary Jane had to be kidding. Now we know he doesn't. Kid."

"You're damn well right he doesn't kid," said Susan. "I haven't learned much by going out with him—but that much I have learned."

"What were they playing?" Cybil asked.

"They were playing three-card monte for Peyton Wood's Canwood stock. He was the banker—he put it on the table for one twenty-five a share. He was selling out, you see—in a way, he was selling out to the highest bidder...."

"But Bobby Finster hasn't money like that," said Susan.

"Bobby wasn't playing. Mary Jane and Gordon Perry were playing. They'd each bought in for half the stock.

Whoever won the game would end up with Peyton Wood's controlling shares."

Cybil coughed and spluttered. She wanted, somehow, to cry, which baffled her. *But all that money—controlling interest—in a card game....*

"Excuse me," she said. And left the table.

She crossed the room and Peter and Susan were under the impression she had gone out into the hall—when, suddenly, she turned around and shouted at them: "WHO ARE THESE BASTARDS? WHY DOESN'T SOMEBODY KILL THEM?"

And then she ran out into the hall and up the stairs where she locked herself in one of the guest rooms.

Susan started to follow her, but Peter, who was thinking of marrying Cybil Torrance once he was divorced from Claire, said: "No. Don't go. She wants to be alone. Her father has just discovered he hasn't half the money he thought he had and she's distressed...."

A moment later, he explained to Susan: "Clearly, there can be no doubt that Mary Jane cheated. I saw him do it, myself. I said nothing—ever the diplomat—but Bobby couldn't restrain himself, and there you have it. Finito."

Susan looked at him.

"I wish you hadn't said that," she said.

At about 5.30 AM they all assembled in the living-room. All, that is, but Bobby Finster and Mary Jane Powell.

Alex Peyton Wood had agreed, because of his military background, to act as referee. The seconds had been appointed—and were now with their men in separate parts of the house. Mary Jane's seconds were his brother Tom and Brian Gossage. Bobby's seconds were Cybil Torrance, who had now regained her composure and was not the least bit angry any more, but calm and resolute. Cybil was joined, on Bobby's side, by the man called Orenstein—mostly because he wanted somehow, even symbolically—to pull the trigger on Mary Jane Powell.

"We must all go down together," Alex Peyton Wood was saying in his reediest of voices. "I believe it is best if all of us are witness to this event. That way, nothing can be distorted. We have chosen Cluny Park as the scene of our little adventure simply because it is there." He smiled and took out a pair of darkly tinted glasses. "Also, of course," he added—once his glasses were in place and he looked the perfect linesman for a tennis match—"it is flat, it is self-contained, and it is private."

And with that, he dispersed them all toward the rear of the house.

"Come along, gentlemen," he called out to Bobby and to Mary Jane. "The moment has arrived!"

*When we were children,* Claire was thinking, *Margot Peyton Wood and I would come down here to Cluny Park and smoke forbidden cigarettes and sit beneath these trees and read the dirty bits from* Peyton Place *and....*

The path gave out before they had reached the bottom. Andrew had put up a chain-link fence that was eight feet high and partly overgrown with wild Virginia creeper and deadly nightshade. A gate pushed outwards—difficult to open because of all the frozen fallen leaves that had blown against the fence.

Alex Peyton Wood was the first one through the gate once Andrew had kicked and pushed and shoved it open. Andrew stayed in place till everyone had passed.

No-one spoke. It was like a silent film. Even Mary Jane was silenced. Claire was watching the back of his head where it rose above the collar of his greatcoat. She was trying to remember what it had been like to love him. There had been so little time for love before she hated him—and she knew that this had been the way it was for all his women. Still, she had no pity for him now. There wasn't a chance in hell that he'd be killed.

The park gave off a rush of silence. Nothing moved but the falling snow and the sight of it was mesmerizing. Each of the figures standing against the backdrop of hillside trees was momentarily stilled as they might have been in one of John Dai Bowen's photographs.

*Eighteen people in evening dress and snowflakes the size of quarters and here I am without my camera....*

"Gentlemen."

Peyton Wood's voice was like a voice inside a tea cup—audible and crisp, but small. He wore his overcoat loosely round his shoulders and took his handkerchief out of his pocket in order to wipe his glasses. He beckoned to the seconds and asked them as a formality if they had made the appropriate attempts to dissuade the duellists from their chosen course of action. "Yes. Yes. Yes," he was told. And, "Yes." The four went back to their appointed places.

The distance between the two men was to be twenty paces when they fired. Each gun was loaded with a single clip—each clip containing a single bullet. One shot each and, whatever the outcome, that would be the end of it.

"Gentlemen, are you ready?"

"Yessir."

"Yes."

"Come forward please," said Peyton Wood. "I want you back to back where I have drawn this line." He had drawn the line with his walking stick—and once Mary Jane and Bobby Finster were standing in their places, shoulders touching and their shirt sleeves grazing as they dropped their arms to their sides. Peyton Wood called out in a kindly way, as if to children at a summer picnic when the fireworks are about to start, "Ladies and gentlemen—please clear the lines of fire...I thank you."

Just before Peyton Wood began the count, Hazel Cournoyer and Fabiana Holbach, standing some ten or twelve feet apart, decided in the instant to raise the umbrellas they had snatched before they left the house. They were like two black, sudden flowers and Cybil Torrance closed her eyes. She held a deep belief in signs, and what this sign might mean was all too clear.

"I shall now commence the count," said Peyton Wood. "And *one*..."

Bobby Finster wanted not to look like an awkward fool, but he felt like an awkward fool—with both arms tight against his sides and his knees locked tight against the jarring of the paces....

"*seven, eight, nine, ten*..."

Alan Northey was thinking, *this will make the most interesting conversation piece when I get back home. Who will believe that I've been to a real live duel?*

"...*twelve, thirteen, fourteen, fifteen*..."

Claire thought, *well—I have to watch this, don't I. For Margot's sake, if not for mine.*

An oak leaf fell from one of the trees and before it touched the ground, the count of twenty had been reached.

Somebody cried out, "Don't!"

Bobby Finster raised his arm and, just as he was pulling his opponent up along his sights, a snowflake landed on his glasses, blinding him.

Someone started laughing wildly.

Bobby Finster fell down. Dead.

Later, much later that morning, someone was pushed, or jumped or fell from the Glen Road bridge. Male. Caucasian. Sandy hair. Hazel eyes. Five foot eleven. Wearing evening clothes.

That he had been shot was not immediately evident, due to the damage done to his head by the fall. This news came later, at the Coroner's. Several police went scrambling amongst the fallen leaves and branches beneath the bridge and, in due course, after perhaps an hour and fifteen minutes of diligent searching, one of them found the Luger with which the fatal shot had been fired.

On the Monday morning, the two men who lived at number one Beaumont Road, at the end of the bridge, were questioned about the previous day and one of them, dressed in a handsome bathrobe, said that—yes—there had definitely been a shot on the Sunday morning, but the man had concluded it was just a motorcar.

So this was the official rendering of Bobby Finster's death—and the one that Margot Finster had delivered to her door.

Stood on the bridge—etcetera—shot himself—etcetera—fell to his death—etcetera—all while of unsound mind.

That, barring Christmas, was how the decade ended. Two weeks and two days after Bobby Finster's death, the nineteen-eighties began.

# Staircase Descended

**George Bowering**

I opened my eyes or I open my eyes and thought or think it
was or is morning. That is a terrible sentence to begin with.
I take it back. I open my eyes, usually, and think it might be
morning. How do you know? Your, no, my glasses are on
the top of the bookcase, and so is the clock with its red
numerals and they tell the time. But can they be said to tell
the time if there is no-one in the room who is capable of
reading the numerals? That is not the kind of question one,
yes that's a good one, one—one wants to ask or even answer

first thing in the morning. If it is morning.

One wants to stay in bed, of course, and to hell with the time of day. But one is also predisposed to getting out of bed. For me that is a problem, the first one of the probable day. Here is the problem: when I wake up I am lying on my right side, knees as close to my chest as possible, one hand under the pillow or rather my head because the pillow has fallen to the floor, there is no pillow. The other hand, who knows? It could be pulled up under my chin. My knees as close to my chest as possible. When I was young I could tuck my knees right up against my chest. No more. But of all the things I cannot make my body do any more, this business with the knees is the least of my troubles. I can lift the knees a lot closer than most men or even women my age, I will wager.

The problem is getting my body out of bed. I do not mean a slacking of the will. I mean that when I wake, nearly blind eyes looking at a red blur of unknown numerals, my body is locked in that position I was so carful to describe just a moment ago. And mind you, I am sick and tired of description. If I go on with this I might have some difficulty with description. I might not do it. You will not find me throwing around adjectives, in any case. I hate the god-dammed slithery unnecessary corruptive willful Anglo-Saxon self-satisfied secondary stylish things. Ha, just a little joke there, you dont mind? To hell with you too. Just fooling.

Trying to get that body out of bed. It might help if I described the bed, but I wont. The body is locked in place by a small imperfection low down in the vertebraic column. If the body lies in roughly the same position for a given period of time, as for instance when I am asleep, it is next to impossible to change its attitude. For instance I cannot induce it to lie on its back and stretch its legs straight toward the so-called foot of the bed. Nor can I swing the legs over the side of the bed, though my body lies on the edge, not in the middle of the bed. It is a medium-wide bed. My father died in it, and there was a woman who used to find room for her body beside mine. In those days my body did not lie in the same position all night.

Many people get out of bed by swinging their legs together, rotating on their buttocks, perhaps, and allowing their trunks to be levered to a vertical position as their heels fall to the floor, where there may be cold wood or gritty linoleum or a warm wool carpet. A warm wool carpet. If there were a warm wool carpet in this room I might sleep on it, and avoid this problem of getting out of the bed. But then the problem of rising vertical from the carpet might be even more daunting. I return to the appropriate problem. I wished and I wish that I could rotate and rise, my heels falling on whatever is down there, sometimes it is hard to remember all these things. That is connected to my dislike of description, I am sure. If I find that I cannot remember something that one would never imagine forgetting, anyone's forgetting, one wants to crawl under the covers if he can find them, and go back to sleep, if you can call what I do sleeping.

Not that I dont try the various ways of getting up in the morning. It is impossible, thank goodness, to describe the feeling when one wants to get up but the body will not do it. It is not the same thing as wanting to move your arm when you wake up with your arm asleep over your head. You begin to move your left leg, let us say, and a signal arrives saying that you will soon be in great familiar pain without hope of gaining some movement at its cost. Hopeless. The signal comes from the small place in the lower region of the sacroiliac, you remember that word. It was very popular in radio-show jokes in the late forties.

So here is what I do—I could list all the ways I fail every morning, but I cannot summon the energy to try to remember them, and if I miss out a few I will not be proud enough of my list, knowing that you will then think that things are not really as bad as all that. Well, why should I care about that? It is too late now, anyway. Here is what I wind up doing. With extremely small movements I nudge the body closer to the edge of the bed. This nudging is meticulous and painstaking and would seem to be hopeless of success if I had not done it on previous occasions. First I might point the big toe on my top, that is right, foot toward the bookcase and move the foot a bit. Then the lower or right shoulder. Then, with the long bony loose-skinned fingers, damned description, of both hands wrapped around the corner of the edge of the mattress, I manage to bounce the round bony ball of my right hip an inch or is it a centimetre over, to the right, that is. You will just have to imagine, if you can summon your faculties better than I can mine, how long this procedure goes on and with what discomfort I must continue it. It makes my body sweat, which is amusing, because my body affords a comparison with the denuded skin of a mature chicken, and one has never seen a chicken perspire, no matter what other discomfiting things one has seen a chicken do. Sweating like that every morning or whenever it is I get out of bed, and yes I finally do, I wish momentarily for a shower. Place of potential disaster. Enough, and more.

Enough. If I do not get at it I will never tell you how I get out of bed and thus solve the first problem of the day. And why bother getting up, you ask. I do not get up. After enough edging and pointing and minute hopping with my frozen shut body I manage to propel myself so far to my right that I achieve the edge and more of the bed. Of course I have not been able to rotate on my hips as we would all like to, but I do turn as I depart the bed, and fall face downward on the floor. There is no stopping me then, not till I come to rest on whatever that surface is. Of course, I always remember if I am jolted enough. It is hardwood, nice dark boards of hardwood. Once they shone, a rich dark brown lateral glint of—no. There is a bang, of course, when I cease falling, and even though I have my hands in position to prevent my face from striking the hardwood, I do land nice and crisp on my knees and elbows, and so the tight grip thus far maintained by the little spot of imperfection in my vertebraic column is slackened just a little. Enough so that in my present position I can begin a careful crawl toward the toilet.

2

Sometimes it is a crawl and sometimes it is more like a creep, a creeping, let us say, to avoid vulgar ambiguity. It would be nice just to stand up and walk or at least hobble to the bathroom, and on the odd occasion I can do just that, if there are enough objects or close enough walls on the route I fall into so that I can support myself on something. There are times when I start by standing up, having pulled myself up the brass leg of the bed, but have to collapse to the hardwood again because the first step or shuffle, let us say, brings a serrated knife blade, this is a fanciful description, you understand, into the small of my back. A small that is the largest thing in my attention at the time. Poor jest, but necessary.

I proceed, embarrassed a little, I mean here is a grown, perhaps, man, on his hands and knees (if it is one of my lucky mornings) crawling out of his bedroom into the hallway and, turning a little to the left, into the bathroom. If you are a man, or at least a man a little like me, you know that in the morning there is a compulsion you cannot shake. In fact it is often the agent that gets you out of bed in the first place. This is the unnegotiable necessity of passing water. Some people are lucky: they hop out of bed in the morning, perhaps flinging their arms wide of their trunks in a little reminder of elementary school exercises, and hippity hop to the toilet, where they pull it out and piddle away, great creamy suds rising on the sides of the bowl, a nineteen-fifties radio song humming in their heads.

While I am crawling toward the bathroom and then across the bathroom to the convenience, fifteen men in my neighbourhood have done just what I outlined above. I crawl past the sink, along the flank of the bathtub, noticing for the hundredth time that one of its clawed feet has a smear of toothpaste on it, and how did that get there again. It could not, certainly, be the same smear that was there, let us say, last 12 February. But there I am then at the device. There is a certain principle at work now—the more movement I am capable of, the more I am capable of movement. It is as if the knot in my back is melting. In an hour or so I will be walking like a normal man or a normal man with a body made of shredded wheat, as I once quipped to Marsha, a woman you will never hear about again. Here I am. But there is no question of waiting until I can perambulate. Not that it is not a temptation. Just let the bladder go, let it unblad, I suppose you could say, and relax. Reeelaaax, says the voice in my left ear. That is where the devil sits when he has time, my mother once said. Enough about her. There will be no resorting to "motivation" in this account.

There I am. There is no question, then, of pointing Percy at the porcelain. I am committed, you might say if this were more serious, this telling, to telling you the details. The truth is that I could stop right here, and I would not mind. You would probably cheer the abandonment. In fact it is unlikely that you have made it this far. If you have, please sign your initials right here:_____

All right, there I am. I am 186 centimetres in height on the occasions when I can stand up fully. I have never been able to measure the toilet bowl in centimetres, but it is just under fourteen inches in height. All right, I will just tell you and let's forget it. I kneel, full of gratitude that I am there, and hang poor Percy over the hard white lip. On most occasions he has reached by now the condition of hangability. But there are mornings on which he will not retreat from the condition he was found to be in on my waking. I do not know or have forgotten what those neighbours of mine do on such an occasion, but I can tell you what I do. I can tell you but just this once I do not believe that I will.

Flushed not too far from my embarrassed face, the toilet is finished for now, and glad I am of it. Now there is the sink and perhaps the shower. I would like to take a shower every morning. In fact there was a time a few years back when I did, and not always alone, I can tell you. What a ridiculous image, you say. All right then, you will get urine and atrocious posture instead of soapy euripus. Now I simply hope that by the time I am ready for the shower I can stand up in it. There is nothing gratifying about coming to rest on one's hands and knees in the tub and feeling the hard water against one's back. But first the sink. I always feel a little guilty when it comes to the sink. This guilt reaches, as most do, a long way back, into childhood, when one's mother warned one about putting one's weight on the poor sink. Damn. There is something about a bathroom that allows one's mother to sidle into the discussion, the monologue, yes I know. But you are here, aren't you, you did sign in, didnt you?

All right, I pull myself up the sink, like a sickly monkey pulling himself up the bars that imprison him while offering him something to ascend. There you go, a simile, I think. You will not, if I have my wits about me, see another of those. Bad enough that I fell into this so-called present tense. No, I made a promise to myself not to spend all my precious time talking about this talking. If it is talking. It looks more like writing to me. There I go. Okay, a short paragraph. I decided on paragraphs, with you in mind. You might remember that.

Up the sink I climbed. (That felt good. Not the climbing. I mean the tense.) (This will get out of hand. I really must stop that sort of thing right now, no matter what attractive thoughts come to mind.) By now I can bear this, the simulacrum of standing, while leaning heavily on the basin. I can manage to get the stopper in. I didnt use one for years until I had to start paying for my own hot water. The taps on. The object is to wash and then debarbarate the face. Now my 186 centimetres give me a new problem, or rather the revisiting of an old problem. I cannot bend to get my face anywhere near the right altitude for laving. I must spread my feet as far apart as possible, rest my bony forearms on the edge of the porcelain, and do the best I can, bobbing my head for a painful half-second, and throwing water and soap toward my cheeks. This goes on. I want to stop but I have to proceed. I want to stop writing or talking or thinking, but you cannot. You cannot stop thinking if you are not a Himalayan anchorite, and what else is there.

So, eventually one gets a razor in one's hand and eventually manages to make momentary scrapes at the face. It is a little like reaching for a piece of paper that is just out of reach on the floor on the other side of those monkey bars. If you overextend your shoulder and elbow and wrist for a second before they all snap back into their proper proportions, you can make a little scrape at the whiskers and soap if you have the razor at the correct angle. This is how I shave almost every morning. I have thought of growing a beard but I cannot. I have random hairs on my face, no pattern and certainly no carpet. I used to tell myself that this unmanliness was a sign that I was a forerunner of human beings from the future. I read a lot of science fiction in my youth, and time travel was my favourite narrative device. I was going to say something about that but I cannot remember what it was. Let us say that I have shaved.

Perhaps now I can get into the shower. The main reasons one gets into the shower, or the main reasons I do, are my hair and the cleft between my buttocks. Perhaps I can get into the shower and at least lean against the wall.

3

Now we come to the heart of this story. It is a story, dont you agree? Now we come to what I thought of as the whole of the story. I could probably put this a better way if I started all over again. But then what would you have? Probably a well-rehearsed narrative and therefore something you cannot trust. If you think that is literary theory, think again. There is nothing at all literary here, I the least so.

I am now approaching the bottom of the stairs from above. That is, I am descending. Not at all like the royalty

76

those words might make one thing of. I am wearing a pair of slippers so old that I cant remember who gave them to me. One never buys one's own slippers any more than one buys one's own after-shave lotion. They, the slippers, have heels that have been crushed under my own for so long that they would appear to someone who has not yet put on his glasses for the day to be made that way. There are plenty of slippers with no heels to them, you know that. You also know that I am for some reason slow to get to this heart of the story I promised or at least mentioned. I am also, I must tell you, since I started on this dressing of the narrator, wearing my ratty old bathrobe or is it housecoat. It is an item that falls to a level just below my knees, and is belted at approximately the waist. That is all. Under this piece of drab phlegm-green terrycloth, I am as naked and as attractive as a hog hanging in the cold room at Peerless Packers.

Ah, say you, ablutions done and staircase descended, he is now going to perform the comfortably familiar ritual of the morning newspaper and fresh egg. That is, ah say you all this while at the same time saying it looks as if this person is going to force upon me or us a lot more sentences than we need about every moment of his waking and god help us perhaps sleeping life. Not so. At least I hope not so: I did not, I will admit, plan on narrating the getting down out of bed and the getting up to the white bowls. How about this: I think that you can depend on my torpor to protect you from a recounting in the familiar present tense of my whole day, one like the next that they are.

No, this is the point at which you encounter not a fresh egg and a minimal daily, but two women at a kitchen table, drinkers of so much coffee that in an hour they will be taking turns at the downstairs toilet, and expenders of more words in that hour than appear in the missing newspaper. It is not really missing, save from this account. Either it is on the front steps where it has been for five hours, or some child, pauper or dog has made off with it again. If there has been a high wind earlier this morning, its pages will be wet to transparency and wrapped around various bushes or weeds in the yard and the neighbour's yard. The neighbour does not read the newspaper. He is a long-haired youth whose occupation seems to be burglary, judging from the peculiar coming and going of packing cases and trailing electrical cords. But you will not be bothered with him again. I do not even know his name, so I cannot even withhold that from you.

So to those two women sitting at the kitchen table, the way women will, sprawling a little, no, that is not quite right, their bodies relaxed so much that they seem to be saying with their easeful slouch that they own the space. No. I will never get that right, so I will drop the attempt. One might as well commit a lot of description, or lay out a row of similies. Anyway, there they are, the two of them, total weight, let us say of a 150 kilograms, maybe less. The prettier one is the neighbour lady, but the other is smarter. She is the one who is related to me by marriage. She thinks that I am gone, and she has her friend persuaded of that illusion. Sometimes it sounds to me as if she thinks that I am dead and gone; other times it seems as if she is convinced that I am just gone, fled, fallen away. Just disappeared from sight. I do not do everything I could to persuade her otherwise, but I make small attempts in that direction. Why do people call that a direction? Let it stand. I hardly can myself.

They are having one of their usual discussions. This is what the lady of the house says:

"Each thing in itself, then, and its essence are one and the same in no merely accidental way, as is evident both from the preceding arguments and because to *know* each thing, at least, is just to know its essence, so that even by the exhibition of instances it becomes clear that both must be one."

To which her visitor responds:

"Ha ha ha ha. You may be right about that and you may be wrong. You could not prove it by me. All I know is that when my old man wants what he wants I dont want what he wants, essence, well, essence never enters into it. It might have worked differently for you when your old man was around. Might have been essence all over the place. Ha ha ha ha. Far as I know. Ho ho."

Now the woman who lives in this house never condescends to her friends or any stranger. She just assumes that they enjoy the possibility of entering the conversation, when they get the chance to talk, at a level that will be comensurate, that is a useable word here, with the one she is speaking on. So she will continue (ah, the future tense, which no more covers the future than the present tense the present):

"For it has been already shown that the soul of the incarnate deity is often supposed to transmigrate at death into another incarnation; and if this takes place when the death is a natural one, there seems no reason why it should not take place when the death has been brought about by violence. Certainly the idea that the soul of a dying person may be transmigrated to his successor is perfectly familiar to primitive peoples."

"I wish I had known that yesterday when I was at the houseplant sale at Corby's," says her fellow coffee-drinker. "That place was full of primitive people yesterday. Oh my!"

At this juncture I decide to make my presence known. Luckily, I *have* had a shower this late morning, and that stream of hot, nearly steaming, water on the small of my back makes it possible for me to walk, even on a level surface. I generally start with a significant stare at one of the two women. Sometimes the visitor is not there; on that occasion I stare at my close relative, bending my neck down the way a pigeon does when it is contemplating a puddle but wary of a crowd of human feet. Having inaugurated the stare, I lift my left hand to a level with my left nipple, wrist tucked in to trunk, and wiggle the upward-pointing fingers a little. When you do that, trying to make each digit independent of the others, the middle finger, the longest, usually refrains from wiggling. Nevertheless, I hope that it *appears* to be wiggling because its neighbours are so doing. I do not want to be thought to be disguising a rude gesture, even with the palm facing the wrong way. Not yet, in any case.

"There is an unmistakable indication in the text of Sophocles' tragedy itself that the legend of Oedipus sprang from some primaeval dream-material that had as its content the distressing disturbance of a child's relation to his parents owing to the first stirrings of sexuality."

"Stirrings!" exclaimed the neighbour. "It's too bad you never had any children before he departed. My boys are stirring all the time. I tell you I hate cleaning up their room. And sometimes I dont feel at all safe myself!"

You could not say the word *sexuality* to this woman without rousing her. Even sitting still in her chair, forearms on the table between them, she seemed to experience a sea change. Her body seemed to become more rounded, to make rounded areas of shininess in her print dress. Perspiration made her throat glow, and moisture appeared in the edges of hair over her ear. Her mouth would not entirely close when it was relieved of its labour of speech. Moisture shone from her front teeth. Her eyes, which before had been simply brown and cool, now glowed as if all at once connected to the electrical power lying patiently in the wires inside the walls between rooms. The palms of her hands were probably wet. The creases at the backs of her knees were likely sticky. She moved her knees a little farther apart, looking, in all likelihood, for air.

How disappointing. I had intended, as you will have gathered, to spare you that sort of thing. The foregoing description should appear thus:

You could not say the word *sexuality* to this woman without rousing her. Even sitting still in her chair, forearms on the table between them, she seemed to experience a sea change. Her body seemed to become more rounded, to make rounded areas of shininess in her print dress. Perspiration made her throat glow, and moisture appeared in the edges of hair over her ear. Her mouth would not entirely close when it was relieved of its labour of speech. Moisture shone from her front teeth. Her eyes, which before had been simply brown and cool, now glowed as if all at once connected to the electrical power lying patiently in the wires inside the walls between rooms. The palms of her hands were probably wet. The creases at the backs of her knees were likely sticky. She moved her knees a little farther apart, looking, in all likelihood, for air.

You think that you know what you would do in this situation? You have that profound confidence? The universe for you is not a maze with possible beasts at the end of any corridor? I congratulate you on your good fortune. I am without envy. I simply wish to express my joy that there is such a fortunate one among us, and therefore maybe many. Joy is likely too exalted a word. What can I put in its place? I suppose we could agree on satisfaction. All right, my satisfaction. But now you must also allow that it is not for me a simple decision to say or do what I do or did in the above circumstance.

I am not stupid: I know that you are objecting to my silence here. Why, you ask, do I not shout at the women to make them notice and indeed acknowledge my existence and more than that my presence. And while we are at it, why do I not effect another conducting of the senses; that is, why do I or did I not reach out and touch the woman of my choice here? Why not grasp the neighbour lady's thigh or seize a handful of my matrimonial partner's raven hair and pull it, vertically or horizontally about seven centimetres, or to be more certain, fifteen? I do not know whether I will be able to explain this to you. I know that there must be personalities like mine in the world, personalities that have been shaped more or less like mine over all the years of our growing up, albeit like potatoes growing in rocky soil, some of us being compelled to grow around a rock and never to achieve the shape assigned to the potato in the little golden book of west coast gardening. If you happen to be one of those rare but surely extant personalities, you will understand easily why I did not make those auditory or palpatory attempts at communication. In fact it is probable that I would not have to waste breath or ink or whatever I am expending in the explanation. You would intuit and agree, you would find the parallel in your heart, or behind your meek heart. For the others, probably the majority of you, I can try the outline of an explanation. Probably anyone, of any personality, will have a layer, a striation of my condition, if condition is an appropriate word here, and I am reluctant to admit it.

All right, for you, the majority, I will try this. If I were to reach out and touch or grab or caress or pull, whether the pretty one or the smart one, and if I could feel the touch and the recipient could not, I would be, ontologically speaking, in trouble. If she could feel it and I could not, I would be filled with doubt at best. If neither of us could feel it—that is, if my hand went right through, say, the upper leg of the woman from down the street, it could mean any number of things. It could mean that we are both goners or creatures of the imagination, and if so, whose? It could mean that I am dreaming, or at least that one of us is, or if that is not stretching likelihood too far, both of us are. It could be that we are both figures in a fiction whose perpetrator is not paying sufficient attention for the moment. It could mean that this is the general rule of things and that my long-held opinion that matter comes to rest against the surface of matter is in error. The possibilities are not endless, but the end is too far away for the amount of energy I have to spare for postulating its place. Suffice it to say that I am aware of many possibilities that I do not want to prove or have proven for me.

It would be a simple thing to attempt a casual, accidental-seeming touch, if there were not other hints of my non-existence, at least as far as these women and the dimension they were in was concerned; and here I go into some sort of past tense again. If they acknowledged me by sight, and were not just ignoring me but unaware of my being, I could touch them without any but the normal fears, a knuckle to the temple or whatever. But then the touch would be unnecessary, as this explanation would be were I speaking or writing to people who could easily understand my attitude. But because these people seemed not to be able to notice me (and this is not just a singular instance, you must remember) by sight, there was a good chance that they would not notice me by touch because the latter was impossible. If not a good chance, at least a chance. As it is, at least till the present time, I would rather try another time to make them notice me by sight, just *in case* they were ignoring me out of spite. I want to hold onto the illusion, if it is an illusion, that I exist, for a while.

There was another possible explanation that I was going to offer, but now I feel that it would take a considerable feat of memory and thought to bring it to the surface of my brain, and I would rather return now to the narrative, if you will agree that that is what I departed from. Besides, the explanation, for those of you who do not resemble me in the most particular of my traits, would be overlong. It is likely that I would lose you, either in the sentences or from the room.

In the meantime, if that is not a silly thing to say at the preface of this resumption, I am in that other room, let us call it a living-room—requisite number of furniture items, crooked magazines on one of them, and I can see the brace of women through the extra-wide kitchen door, at least it is the kitchen door from my viewpoint. From theirs it is probably the living-room door. It is not really a door, but rather a kind of formality for those who like to know that they are passing between rooms, a kind of minimal archway, really a rounding of the corners, a sort of slight decrease in the distance from wall to wall. Through this thing I will call a door simply for the sake of this narrative, persist in misnaming it, I can see the two women and hear their conversation as suggested above. I mean I dont expect you to believe that I have caught a verbatim series of remarks from one particular afternoon—I am using the present tense from time to time, after all. Really I just went and selected some likely passages from books of an unmistakably intellectual bent.

Now what I do is to remove my clothes. I cannot remember what I said I was wearing, so I will rely on you to remember, or to go back and look it up. Let us say that I was wearing pyjamas, my ratty old striped blue-and-white ones that I have to hold the pants of up unless I am wearing my old greenish terrycloth robe. Well, let us say, or I will, that I was at the moment in question wearing all that stuff. And my bedroom slippers, the ones, I remember now, with the squashed down heels. I take all these things off. No I dont. But I undo the belt of my robe, and then I let the pyjama bottoms drop. I kick off my bedroom slippers in order to kick off the pyjama bottoms that have settled around my feet. Then I can dance.

Here is what the dance looks like. Rather, here is what I imagine the dance to look like; as the dancer I am in no position to observe or reflect on the dance. I hold the skirts of my off-green terrycloth robe in my two hands and lift them sideways, away from my body. Then I contrive to bend my bony legs, knobby, really, they are knobby at the hip, knee, ankle and foot, bend my knobby legs and kick my feet out sideways. All this time I make certain that I am facing the conversation at the kitchen table. I might describe an arc, little part of a semi-circle, there in the adjoining room, but always with the effect of total angular continuity. I dance and dance. I take a chance and kick my bony heel knobs together. My genitals swing back and forth in opposition to my legs. That is, when my legs are kicking left, my genitals are still swinging right. But enough about them. I dont think that my genitals are any funnier or any more an affront than the rest of my white, hairless, smooth, gravity-formed body.

What do I want? Do I want to test the limits of their ability to pretend that I am not there? Am I by now allowing that I might not exist, at least for them, and enjoying a dare otherwise prevented by childhood training in repression and civility? Why dont I approach, why dont I press the advantage that would be granted by proximity? I believe that I have explained that above, at least for those readers or listeners who would benefit by explanation, that is, understand and even, perhaps, sympathize. Now, wouldnt that be grand? Sympathy. I, even were I not after all a literary figure, as I am sure I am for you, one that you may even have grown tired of, would appreciate and welcome sympathy as quickly as the next fellow. But now I was finding it to be as much as I could handle to try for recognition.

How did my audience, if I may have your indulgence in calling them that for the nonce, react to my terpsichorean antics? After I had exhausted myself, and was sprawled out in what had been her father's favourite easy chair, legs extended in front of me, skirts of my robe falling behind each stringy thigh, this is what I heard them to say.

"Diogenes, another follower of Anaximenes, held that air was the ultimate element of all things, but that nothing could be produced from it without the agency of the divine reason, which permeated it. Anaxagoras was followed by his pupil Archelaus. He, too, asserted that everything in the universe was composed of like particles, which, however, were informed by intelligence. This mind, by causing the conjunction and dissolution of the eternal bodies or particles, was the source of all movements."

"I'd have to think for a while to agree about *all* movements. I got a husband, and you dont know how lucky you are sometimes, and two huge boys, and I cant believe that there is any mind behind their movements, especially when they are coming down the stairs, or when they are picking up knives and forks, when I can convince them to use such elementary tools."

I was exhausted. There was nothing more I could do there. I was certainly not going to go into the kitchen to get coffee or a muffin or even a limp piece of broccoli. I did not want to play ghost, because I might start to believe in my own demise. I did not want to touch one of those people. What if I touched one, and she responded in such a way as to show that she had known I was there all the time? One does not like to entertain the notion that one is that little worthy of remark. I would go upstairs, and then I would decide whether to get dressed and go out, thinking of the near impossibility of donning socks, of bending to stick one over a big toe, and if I did go out I would get a cup of coffee and even a lemon-guck-filled danish pastry. I would go to Daphne's Lunch. Everyone knows me there. They say hello and say my name out loud when I enter the premises. They know enough to let me sit at a banquette even when I am using a table for four, because of my bad back. I am visible there. I do not know the names of any of the waitresses or the regular patrons I see there every time I attend. But we are a community. A community of laggards, perhaps, but a *polis*.


4


Perhaps you will agree that that scene, with the two talkative women and the dancing geezer, was the heart of this story, given that you have already acceded to the notion that this is a story. What, then, will we call the following. The following scene, perhaps a kind of loosening of the knot we have got ourselves tied in, takes place in Daphne's Lunch, where you will not hear saints and thinkers dis-

cussed all that often. Oh, once in a while I will quote Hera-
clitus to some hapless toiler for the minimum wage. But in
general, philosophy is not broached there. Until today. Or
that day. Let us say today.

Today I found myself talking with an old gent who
seemed to admire his ability to pick a teabag out of its cup
and suspend it over its home in such a way that the drips of
tea will fall into the centre of the red-brown liquid. No, I
*find* myself talking with him. I do not know his name, and I
do not think that he knows mine. It is in such circumstances that one may find oneself these days. There is a little
ambiguity for you, I mean that sentence. But you knew
that, didn't you? All right, I will get on with this tale. Nice
day. Nice day. Havent seen such nice weather this time of
year in years. Last year we were soaking wet and cold as hell
this time of year. This kind of weather is good for your
rheumatism. Good for what ails you. You bet. Wouldnt
mind being 30 years younger all the same. You bet, I would
settle for twenty.

And so on. I know how to tailor my conversation for this
crowd. It never strikes me that the guy I am talking with
might be tailoring this conversation for this crowd, with
me as part of this crowd. Who knows? We may, if we were
to meet somewhere else, say one of the conference rooms at
the Regency Hotel, have begun a discussion of Anaxagoras
and his tradition. Be that as it may, we got onto a discussion
of ontology or the like anyway. How we got there from the
quite ordinary weather, I do not recall. Or I do not want to
write or say it out. Eventually I got most of the lemon-gunk
into my mouth and some on my lap, and was in conversation. I could end this account right here, and not make it
any the less inconclusive that it is going to be. You will say
that you would have liked to be warned of that at least

around page four. Well, here is your chance. You can drop it right now, leave the beanery, browse the bookstore, two blocks east, cross the street, find an uplifting story of a meaningful fiction. Let me suggest the paperback edition of Michael Ondaatje's *Running in the Family*. Even if you dont buy it, you will have avoided the following conversation.

"My wife cant see me."

"You too?"

"She looks right through me."

"They are like that. That is why they are wives."

I let him sip his tea. I allowed the waitress to refill my coffee cup. I had to think about this. How will I relate to this gent who doubtless has a name but one that does not hang in the air between us, a story that will not be instantly convertible into the clichés of figurative language surrounding connubial friction?

"She thinks that I am dead. Or if not that, she is of the opinion that I have in some less mortal way retired from the site of our domicile. She thinks that I am no longer there."

"Sounds just like my wife, bless her departed soul."

Back there, I think, in the heart of the story, I cannot persuade anyone of my existence, much less my propinquity. Now my appearance, in such an habitual location, is unquestioned. I can now not speak the opposite. I cant persuade someone of my absence, my non-being, albeit only in the eyes, or rather out of the eyes and mind of another, or in this case two others, at least.

It strikes me that this gent without the name may think that he is only speaking with a revery, only imagining this conversation, imagining that there is a coffee-drinking fellow with a bad back with whom he is in conversation. It is late morning. Old bones rest and old brains enjoy their little trips.

"Have a look at me," I say.

People dont, as a rule, like to do that in places like Daphne's. They usually let their eyes flit. To the waitress as she turns her back and carries something to the kitchen hole. To the passing balloon outside the window, a kid has been to a celebrating bank. To the widow at another table. She is smoking a cigarette and reading a small paperback novel placed inside a leatherette cover. But this fellow does look now.

"Am I looking at anything in particular?" he says.

"Can you see a scar on my face?"

He looks.

"Yes I can."

"Where is it?"

"Well, there are two. There is a small one right at your hairline above the middle of your forehead, and there is a slightly longer one that runs from the corner of your mouth down at a 45° angle."

It was more like a 30° angle, but I let it go.

"Thank you."

All right, I do exist. At least in this circumstance, in this environment, I exist.

"So to you I am visible," I suggest.

"Sure. Unless you are not supposed to be here. If your wife calls I will say I havent seen you, if you want."

"No, no. That's not what I mean. She would never phone this place anyway. Nor would she enter it willingly. She goes to well-lit places where they serve little things on croissants for $7."

All right, I have settled the question of whether he is imagining me. There is still the question about whether I have created him. If he is a product of my imagination, there is not all that much currency in his attestation that he can see me as well as talking with me.

It strikes me that I could just rest comfortable, take everything at face value. But it also strikes me that I am not any better off than I was in the living-room of my own house, except that I am enjoying a second cup of coffee. There I was pretty well convinced of my presence; I was propriocepting quite handily, thank you. But others were not reflecting knowledge and awareness of my corporeal entity. Here I receive outside attestation of my being and presence, but I feel the possibility of uncertainty as to whether I have not generated, mentally, of course, the agent of that corroboration.

I should, perhaps, as they say, have stood in bed.

Maybe I did. But no, I cannot accept that. I cannot allow that all that pain of rising for the dubious day was nothing, or for nothing. Or that it will be if I do it. I do not want to spend a life made from now on and who knows how long till now, made entirely of mentation. Of course all you can receive through the agency of this expenditure of words is something that resembles mentation more than it does any more physical and palpable action, if we can speak of action rather than the thing acting as palpable. Maybe I dont even palpate anything any more. Did I just imagine being downstairs and dancing? Am I not now sitting on a reddish banquette at Daphne's, thinking of my hard bed as down that street, up those stairs? Is there anyone reading or hearing this?

# The More Important Things

**Rohinton Mistry**

The large round biscuit tin was deep, and full of marbles. I slid my hand softly into it. They trickled over my fingers. It was like water without wet. A quiet splashing, clinkling sound. But if the hand moved too much or suddenly, then the marbles rattled against the side of the tin, and the sound was like money, and louder.

My father made that noise when he came home from tuning pianos and dropped his change in his old tin. That sound was not nice. The tin said Panama Cigarettes, and was rusted. The sound was clangy and harsh, the way my father spoke whenever his breath smelled of that thing called *feni,* which he drank next door till late at night with Lancelot Braganza. But sometimes, even the money sound was not bad if he came home early. The best days were when he bought *The Illustrated Weekly of India* and sat to read it; now and then he stopped to tell us interesting things from it.

The tin used to be new and shiny. Once, when I had nothing to do, I took a piece of sandpaper and removed all the rust, but in a few days the brown coating had come back. My father said this was because the tin was not galvanized, since cigarette tins were meant to be thrown away when they were empty, though when he was a child he had watched his father (Tony, I am talking about your grandfather, he explained) save his loose change in a cigarette tin too, and if it was good enough for Grandpa DeCosta, it was good enough for Desmond DeCosta; and who had the money to afford anything fancier?

I knew what galvanized meant. It was named after Luigi Galvani. I had learned it in my General Science class. The Science master, Mr. Lalvani, had made a joke: "Remember that name, it rhymes with mine. Only one important difference which no-one must forget: Luigi was Italian, I am Punjabi."

Punjab was in the north, very far from Bombay. It used to be one big state, and then the Hindus and Sikhs were fighting, so in November 1966, Prime Minister Indira Gandhi divided it into two, Haryana for Hindus and Punjab for Sikhs, said the Social Science teacher.

Mr. Lalvani did not wear a turban. He had no beard either. So he must be Hindu. But then why did he say, I am Punjabi? It was very confusing. The Social Studies teacher did not explain that. Maybe that's why my father used to say that education today was hopeless.

I wondered if they played marbles in Punjab and Haryana. Punjab and Haryana, and Himachal Pradesh, were the northernmost states, next to Kashmir, said the teacher. Very cold, and it even snowed there. Just like a foreign country. They could not play marbles on snow. My mother's sister lived in Himachal Pradesh. My auntie. She had two sons, and they were my cousins, but I had never met them because they lived so far away. It took two days and nights on the train to get there, and it was very expensive. There was a photograph in which they were wearing woollen caps and scarves and sweaters, just like a foreign country.

I moved my fingers slowly, and the marbles rolled and trickled over them. One fell out. I picked it up. Its colour was exactly like the uniform that the *jawans* of the Indian Army wore.

When India and China were having a war, everyone was worried for auntie and her family, because they were so close to the frontier, and the newspaper said that the Chinese hordes were simply pouring in. All the papers said India had tried for peace, and would keep on trying; slogans like "Hindi-Chinee *bhai-bhai*" were popular at first, but if the Chinese did not want to be brothers with us, Pandit Nehru said "*Dushman ko hata doe.*" That was what the Indian Army was doing, removing the enemy, although the Chinese hordes were simply pouring in anyway.

I wriggled my fingers gently inside the tin again. The marbles moved and rolled and plashed, like glassy, magical, colourful water. If someone was watching, they would think I was silly. But they did not know what was in my mind. It was my colourful galaxy. The galaxy was made up of countless solar systems, and each solar system had a sun at the centre which was really a huge, huge bright star, and the planets moved around it, and in our solar system there were nine planets whose names were Mercury, Venus, Earth, Mars, Jupiter, Saturn, Uranus, Neptune and Pluto.

The marbles made me forget about the other things I wanted, and did not have, like a drawer in my father's big black desk where Edwin and Alice each had one, an electric torch, a Meccano set, a bicycle. It was better to forget about these things, because I would never get them. But sometimes it also felt exciting to dream and make plans about what I would do with them if I did.

Except for the marbles, everything I had used to belong to Edwin or Alice. My father and mother said there was not enough money to buy new things for everyone. But last year on my birthday I got a new school uniform. I was eight years old. Eight complete, and running nine. Why running? If it was, why did it not come sooner than the previous one? It was just a way of talking. Maybe for Mr. Lalvani too it was just a way of talking when he said, I am Punjabi, even though he had no turban or beard.

Edwin's old uniforms lasted a long time. But my father said they were a gone case now. The collars had been reversed once, and now even the other side was torn. The white stuff inside, which used to make the collar stiff and poke into your neck but later became soft after it had been washed many times, was falling out. And the seats of the short pants had holes in them. My mother tried very hard to save them. "Go to sleep now, Maria," my father said, "or you will go blind." But she sat up late, trying to mend the collars and seats, while he went to bed. She kept moving the cloth and touching her spectacles. First she brought the collar very close to her face, then moved it back a little, then brought it close again. "My number has changed," she said, "but when the wedding season is going strong again, there will be a big demand for bands. They will need their pianos tuned." She gave the needle and thread to me. "Then Desmond will earn a bit more and I can buy new ones." I licked the thread to make it stiff, and put it through the hole in one shot.

I wished she would stop and go to bed. She removed her glasses, rubbed her eyes, and wore them again. I wondered if the clothes would look okay when she finished. The teachers in my school, especially the Fathers, were very strict about uniforms. Some of them were really mean, they called you to the front of the class and embarrassed you: "What is your excuse? *Dhobi* did not wash your new uniform on time?" They would look at the boys sitting quietly, some of whom would laugh nervously because their own uniforms were also shabby. "If you are going to dress like a *ghati,* better go to some municipal school, don't come here." Then there was more laughing.

Alice was lucky. She never had to wear anyone's old uniforms. Sometimes, my father said that three boys would have been so much easier with clothes, the way it was with textbooks.

My Radiant Reader had several names inside the cover. The first one was Ramesh Chopra. Whoever he was, his parents must have been rich, to buy a brand new textbook. Ramesh Chopra had been cancelled and Edwin DeCosta was written instead. Then Alice below Edwin, and finally Tony. It was the same with the other textbooks, except for the first name. In my history book, the list started with Iqbal Mohammed, and the arithmetic text was Jasbir Singh's. The ghosts of these strangers were inside the textbooks too, they could not be left behind just by turning the cover. On some pages, paragraphs were underlined, with notations in the margin, such as "imp." or "v. imp." or "learn by heart" or "sure for final exam." Sometimes, large sections had a curly bracket that said "omit" or "not imp."

These people were still living inside my books, telling me what to read and what to skip, and my eyes obeyed even though I did not really want to. Reading the books of strangers made me feel that I was the real stranger. The books also had different smells from different school bags in which they had lain for a year at a time. It took a while before those odours were replaced by the omelet sandwich and Britannia Marie Biscuit smell of my own bag.

But my poetry book was different. I liked it from the very beginning. There were not many markings in it, and the smell was nice. It was soothing, like some of the poems in the book. Maybe it was reading those poems that made me imagine the soothing smell. The poem I liked best was about Winkyn, Blinkyn and Nod. Or Wynkin, Blynkin and Nod. The spelling was tricky. When I got wet in the rain sometimes, and then came home and dried myself with a towel and put on dry clothes, I felt like Winkyn, Blinkyn and Nod. The best part was taking off the shoes and turning them upside down so all the water ran out, and the socks, which I squeezed till more water ran. The greater the quantity of water, the more heroic I felt for having survived the storm. Then I rubbed my feet with the towel and put on my slippers.

That poem always made me warm, especially if I read it in bed. And the marbles did the same thing. In my friends' hands at school they were dull and ordinary. But something happened after I brought them home and washed and wiped them. It was almost magical. Though books were not, marbles were like money, because when beggars got moeny, it became their own, even if it used to belong to a *lakhpati* with six cars.

I never begged for marbles, though. My friends in school gave them to me. They said I brought them good luck. It started one day when I was just standing and watching. It was a game of Triangles, and there were lots of marbles inside the triangle. The winner would take them all. It was scratched in the dirt of the playground. It should have been an equilateral triangle but was not, because in an equilateral triangle the three sides had to be of equal length, and all three angles were 60° each, and the sum of the angles of any triangle added up to 180°.

That day I had ten paise. For ten paise you could purchase one large shooter marble and five small ones for betting. Patla Babu and Jhaaria Babu sold them near the school gate. Sometimes Patla squeezed your bum and then gave you one more, free.

But I did not buy them. These fellows were all experts, and I had never played before, ever. Trying new things scared me. I just stood and watched. Then one of them asked if I would hold his extra marbles that were not inside the triangle. His name was Dilip and he was in my class, so I said okay, and soon he won the game. He was very pleased, and gave seven to me as a gift. "You brought me good luck, *yaar*," he said.

The next day, I was again just watching when Dilip repeated his request. He gave me ten marbles after winning this time, and called it *baksheesh*. I think using that word made him feel like a grownup. We made a deal: ten every day for me if I stood and helped him during short recess and long recess.

My mother gave *baksheesh* to the sweeper on Christmas. She used to give 50 paise, but then the government did devaluation, and everything cost more, so after that she gave one rupee. The sweeper never made mistakes about *baksheesh.* On Christmas he went to Christian homes, and on Diwali to Hindus. For Pateti, he went to Parsees because they were celebrating their new year. The sweeper knew all the festivals.

The short recess was only twenty minutes long. The whole of it went in going to the bathroom. There was a Hindi master who terrorized us. He threatened that he would "beat you till you do *peshaab* in your *puttaloon* if you misbehave." No-one believed this. Then one day we saw the Hindi master slap a boy, who did wet his pants. When we asked the boy later, he said it was almost automatic, that as soon as the Hindi master raised his hand the piss came out. A few drops first, then the whole stream.

So I always wanted to be sure that I was never full. The bathroom was at the back of the school. There was a row of urinals, and behind them, a row of stalls. I avoided the stalls since my first day of school when I had wandered by mistake to the back, in search for a vacant urinal. The stench from the stalls was much worse than the urinals; once it got into your nose, it filled up your whole head, and then you smelled the stink all day. I hoped that I would never have to go for number two at school. In the rainy season the floors were wet and slippery. I was afraid that I would skid and fall into foaming piss, into the churning, bubbling, smelly river of the urinals. There was a song called "Yellow River" that was played very often on Radio Ceylon on the morning program, Musical Clock. It was my brother's favourite program. When that song came, he made the radio louder, and at once my father shouted, "You want to make us all deaf or what, Edwin?" and my mother quickly went to make it quiet. That song was special, said Edwin, it was very important because it was about the Vietnam war. North Vietnam was fighting with South Vietnam. I felt that that was worse than the India-China war. It would be like North India fighting with South India, my auntie and my cousins fighting me and my parents.

But every time I heard "Yellow River" it reminded me of the stinking school bathroom. To make it worse, when your turn came, the boys waiting behind you in line pushed you in the small of your back and played the fool, making the arc of piss shake and swerve, and if you did not hold it skilfully, it wet your pants. This had happened once to me, and I had had to sit in class with the clammy cloth glued to my thigh, which first felt warm, and then became very cold. I felt so ashamed and miserable, and had to listen to all their teasing on top of it: "Ask your mummy to aim it straight for you" or "sit and do it, if your hole is like a girl's." After that day, I waited till the rush in the bathroom finished before I went in, which was usually at the end of the short recess.

But my new friend, Dilip, helped me to find a safe spot. He was taller and stronger than I. He stood behind, guarding the rear. The whole thing was quicker now, and fifteen of the short recess' twenty minutes were saved for marbles.

Everyone who played marbles wanted my help. They believed that if I held their marbles, they would win. "Tony's hand has magic," they said, "he brings good luck." Someone who was in a higher standard called me Tony the Talisman, and from then on that was my nickname. But I had to look up the meaning in the dictionary.

I was able to choose who I would help, and I kept changing. Everyone said that was the fairest way of doing it, so the same fellow would not have good luck all the time. But I really did it because I had seen that the same fellow never kept winning. It was safer to work with the law of averages.

Lancelot Braganza who lived next door to us believed in the law of averages. He was once talking about Matka numbers to my father. They were standing outside by the stairs. He said he had a system. It was a safe system because it was based on the law of averages, he said. Then my father told me to go inside and not listen to big people discussing things unsuitable for children.

I wished that my marbles came in the real way, by playing and winning. But everyone believed in me now. They believed in me holding their marbles as much as my mother believed in lighting a candle at Mount Mary in Bandra. Even when someone lost, they did not blame me but found another reason.

The biscuit tin soon filled up. Now I could come home and sink my hand in it. The marbles rubbed against my fingers and slipped between them. It felt best when they touched the soft part at the bottom of the fingers, near the palm. When I first put my hand in the box, the marbles felt cool, but soon they became warmer and, after a while, wet and sticky with my sweat. This felt unpleasant and nice all at the same time. I could hear my father laughing and joking next door in Lancelot Braganza's flat, drinking that stinking *feni*. Later on there were always fights between my mother and my father. But the sound of marbles made the sound of shouting less ugly. And the angry faces of my parents disappeared behind the brilliant colours, as I thought about the day at school and all the marble-playing.

The game was best during long recess, which lasted a whole hour. I spent ten minutes on lunch and the rest with my marble-players. It used to take longer before, when my mother sent lunch with the tiffin-carrier. I had to find a place in the lunchroom, which sometimes took a while, and the rice was steaming and I had to blow on it, which took more time, but not as much as it would if I waited for it to cool by itself.

When my father came at night from Lancelot Braganza's flat, he always complained that the dinner was too hot. It was a waste of time, he said, to sit at the table and just wait for the food to cool enough so it would not burn his mouth. He said that not only time was wasted but also the gas, burning away while the food boiled and boiled, hotter and hotter.

Then my mother started working at the export company because the money from piano-tuning wasn't enough. So she packed a dry lunch for me. I preferred it this way, sandwiches could be eaten standing anywhere on the playground.

Everyone at home was surprised that I had such a lot of marbles. I felt bad about telling how I got them. So when my father said to my mother, his voice sounding very proud, "Well Maria, your son is becoming a crackshot marble player," I did not say anything. It made me feel uncomfortable, like the hard collar of my new school uniform had last year, but which became softer and stopped bothering me after the *dhobi* washed it a few times. The undeserved praise also fit better after a while. I began enjoying it.

That year, marbles became more popular in school than they had ever been. It began to worry the school authorities. During a meeting of the PTA, someone said in a speech that "the problem had assumed endemic proportions." It was reported in the school's monthly newspaper. I did not always read that, but this time there was a whole page about the marble problem. There was some rubbish in the beginning, and then the good part:

During the recesses, the playground is populated by groups who gather around a triangle in the dust, or a rectangle for *khoibar*, or the *gull* dug in the ground, an inch in diameter and depth, for the simple and puerile routine of *Raja-Rani*. All faces are turned downwards, no-one looks at the sky anymore; heaven has been repudiated for hell. The library and gymnasium, those noble institutions that nurture our youth for the more important things in life, and make them grow into the fine upstanding citizens that our country is so much in need of, are perpetually deserted. Other games like football, hockey, table-tennis and badminton, which are indeed essential for the well-rounded development, are vitually forgotten. And even that prince of all games, that epitome of sportsmanship, which is not only an art but also a science, namely cricket, has passed out of favour.

The craze for marbles has ramifications outside the playground and beyond the short and long recesses. When the boys change classes between periods, filing out for PT, or Visuals, or according to their choice of Gujarati or Marathi for Second Language, the corridors are filled with a new sound. The tramping of feet is accompanied by the jingling of marble-loaded pockets, and the air is coloured by a chhung-chhung rhythm.

This abomination must cease. This pastime of street urchins, this wasteful activity that is fit only to fill the time of the uneducated and the ignorant, is not worthy of the students of this great institution. Henceforth, the vile disease must be expunged, driven out from within these hallowed halls.

My boys, heed the call of your Alma Mater and your country. Turn again to the finer things in life that will stand by you faithfully, to steady your rudders and fill your sails as you voyage upon the sea of life. Abandon the craze for lowly things that do not help but hinder your growth. Relegate them again to the gutters from which they emerged.

I knew even before I finished reading that it was written by Father Varma, the Vice-Principal. He always used phrases like "prince of games" and "hallowed halls" and "sea of life." He wrote like this whenever something happened which he thought was a big problem that put the school in danger.

Sometimes, a marble fell by mistake in class, during pin-drop silence. It bounced away slowly into a corner. Marbles have a lazy way of bouncing, they always take their time, and this made the teacher more mad. The owner was the big winner that day, whose pockets were very full. He was sent to the Vice-Principal's office for a caning.

Father Varma did it with a ruler instead of the cane that stood in the corner behind his filing-cabinet. Boys who had felt both said the ruler was worse, because Father Varma used the thin edge. Father Varma was from the untouchable class, it was whispered, and he had converted only to escape from it. We privately called him names like *bhunghi* and *harijan*. Some also said that he was a homo, and became a priest so he could be in a boys' school, where thrashing the boys gave him a sexy feeling.

But I was not sure whether to believe everything. Many of the Fathers and Brothers in the school were very strict. Most were vicious when it came to giving punishment, and Brother Tomas was the only one who laughed and joked with us. He was a red-faced Spaniard, in charge of collecting the fees. He also looked after the school's aquarium and the flock of stuffed animals. He had shot the animals himself. It was a strange mixture of duties, but he was a very strong man and could do it all. He was friendly with everyone. During the lunch break he came out on the playground and talked to us. Sometimes he placed his hands flat on his head and let a boy hang from his upper arm, one on each side. He then made his muscles move up and down, so that the boy rose and fell with it. I had done this once and Brother Tomas's sweaty armpit had smelt like vinegar. Some of the senior boys joked that Father Varma did the same thing with his hard catholic cock, made a little kid hang from it and then waggled it.

I liked the sound of the words: catholic cock. They were dirty words, though, and I would never say them at home. But like Tony the Talisman, the sound was nice.

Brother Tomas was the only one who did not mind the marbles. He even liked to watch. But he was not the man in charge. Father Lopez was the principal. He carried around with him a feather duster and the school keys in a hard leather key-case. If he found a boy that annoyed him, he lashed out with the handle-end of the feather duster or knocked him over the head with the leather key-case. Both could hurt very much. Boys who went to Hindi movies said that Father Lopez swung out just like the hero, Dev Anand, did. Every morning, in the stone quadrangle, he led the school prayer at the end of the daily assembly.

One morning, Father Lopez on his wooden platform, looking very tall and strict in his white cassock and black beard, made the sign of the cross to begin. Then the order of the assembly was broken by a marble bouncing on the stone floor. It went rat-a-tat-a-tat-a-tat without ending. It was followed by another, and another; some poor fellow's pocket had got a leak, and all his marbles were slipping out. He tried very hard to stop them but couldn't. He grabbed his pocket from outside, then put his hand inside the pocket to catch the marbles, but it was no use. All went falling on the stone floor.

"The stupid goat whose marbles are falling will come forward right now!" Father Lopez's voice became very shrill. He reached in his cassock for the key-case. The boy left his position and moved slowly to Father Lopez's platform. He was trembling. But the marbles kept falling rat-a-tat-a-tat-a-tat on the stone floor.

"Stop the noise, you goat!" yelled Father Lopez, "Walk faster unless you want to walk out the school gate and never return!" The boy hurried. Then he slowed down and tried to stop the marbles. He slipped his hand up his short pants to find the hole, but he was trembling and couldn't. He hurried again. When he reached the platform, the last marble slipped out at Father Lopez's feet.

"You stupid goat!" said Father Lopez, and raised the leather key-case. But with his arm in mid-air he stopped. He looked just like a film poster of Dev Anand, except for his cassock and beard. The marbles were still bouncing.

"Silly donkeys!" Father Lopez addressed the whole assembly, lowering his arm. "Standing and staring like owls! Catch those marbles and stop the noise! Shameless creatures!" We ran after the bouncing marbles. They were all captured and turned over to Father Lopez. The assembly was dismissed after the school prayer, except for that boy who was taken to the Principal's office.

And that same day, a new rule was announced. All the masters and teachers were told to read the notice aloud to their classes: "No boy is allowed to carry more than five marbles in his pocket. Anyone suspected of breaching the rule may be searched by a teacher or Father or Brother at any time. Punishment will be confiscation of all marbles, caning by Father Varma or Father Lopez and writing, in neat longhand, one thousand times: I will not carry more than five marbles in my pocket."

The new rule made it difficult. And now at home, too, my marbles were not welcome. Suddenly everything was changed. When my mother gave me more biscuit tins to fill, my father said, "Don't encourage the boy, enough is enough." He did not talk about me anymore with pride in his voice.

"What will you do with them all?" he asked me. "There are more important things than marbles."

"But I'm a champion player," I said. The lie came easily. "I could win the world title."

"There's no such thing. Champion nuisance these boxes are becoming, that is all," he grumbled. "If you lose one on the floor someone will slip on it and break their head, I'm telling you."

"I'll be very careful."

"Marbles will not feed your stomach. Champion at studies is what you need to be."

I wondered if there really was a World Marble Championship. But no-one at school knew for sure. We didn't even know if they played marbles in foreign countries. Maybe if the Indian Government made it the national sport, it might begin to spread everywhere.

My father complained more as the boxes grew in number. Then my mother also took his side.

"I didn't want to say it in the beginning," she said, "but marbles bring bad luck. They are as bad as peacock feathers and seashells, never keep them in the house."

"That is right," said my father. "I know what you are saying. Old man Furtado next door told me, the year before he died, about a family in Panjim that was completely destroyed for this reason. When they got rid of the seashells, things began to get better."

Everyone hated marbles. In school, and at home. Why they were against such beautiful things, I could not understand. But I did not pay much attention because the problem in school was bigger.

My friends were wondering what to do with their marbles. For a few days everyone followed the new rule, which was no fun. Then I showed them how to wrap the marbles in a hanky and knot the ends tight to make a little pouch. The marbles sat inside without room to move and rattle. Now all the boys who used to think it was sissy to carry a handkerchief got one everyday. They made their mothers very happy.

Father Lopez was also very happy because the jingle and jangle in classes and corridors stopped, and no-one had to be searched or caned.

Marble-playing started again, and my collection began to grow fast. I spent my time in the evening after school sorting the marbles and counting them. I kept in a separate box the brilliant ones with coloured centres, with curvy swervy squiggles. They were wonderful to look at against the light, and roll between my finger and thumb. Their coloured insides were of different shapes and sizes, and I could imagine them to be anything I wanted, like I did with clouds. The completely transparent ones were called sodas, because that's what they looked like, with tiny bubbles inside, like sodawater.

A few weeks after the new school rule, my father began spending more time at home. He told my mother, "Don't worry what will happen, Maria. Only one piano today." She was home early because the export company was cutting down overtime. All this with devaluation was terrible, they said. So much bad luck could only have one explanation.

"We were right about the marbles," he said to her. I was in the next room. "What to do, just throw them away?"

"Maybe talk to him about what is happening because of the marbles."

"You think he will listen? Your son does not understand. All these days I'm telling him, give some attention to your studies also, but it is like I'm just a dog barking in the night."

Then I couldn't hear anymore because I opened my favourite box and put my hand inside. The marbles rolled around and rubbed against my fingers and I took a handful and shook them, then let them trickle into the box, listening to their sound.

Suddenly something touched my shoulder. It really scared me and I jumped and dropped the box on the floor. It made a loud crash and all the marbles went scattering and bouncing around the room.

My mother felt bad about scaring me, so to cover it up she started scolding: "You didn't hear me talking to you when I came in?"

My father heard the crash and came running. He saw the marbles bouncing toward him. He jumped to one side and clung to the cupboard in the room, as if they were attacking him.

"See? I told you this would happen," he shouted, half-angry and half-worried. "You children don't understand when your parents tell you nicely. You want me to slip on them and break my leg? Hurting it on that stupid broken-up pavement outside was not enough?"

It was a long time after which he had mentioned that again. He had been so unhappy when the pavement outside our building was stolen. The flat stones were taken away and it was never fixed, although he still kept hoping that one day it would. It was covered with mud and little pebbles, all rough and uneven. But it was more fun like this, because now the street sweeper did not clean it every morning, and I found interesting things buried in the dust, like bottle caps from soda or beer, and different kinds of cigarette butts. And at Diwali, the little red firecrackers that smelled of gunpowder. Like a certain type of fart, that smell was, although there was more variety with farts. Faredoon Irani in my class would let one out, then say, "Hardboiled eggs! Hardboiled eggs!" and make us all smell it. Like most Irani boys, he was very tough, and we obeyed him.

I went chasing after the marbles but it was no use. There were too many of them, and it seemed to me as if they knew what they were doing and had made up their minds which way to go. They bounced their way into the other room, past the kitchen and the stoves, past the dining-table and under the crucifix hanging on the wall beside the table, which my father looked at every time he left the house. Actually, we were all supposed to look at the crucifix before going out, but sometimes I forgot, till my mother pointed to it.

The door leading into the hallway was open, and the marbles found their way. We followed them.

Then they began to cascade down the stairs. So many marbles all bouncing down the hollow wooden stairs made a great noise. The din brought out Lancelot Braganza from the flat next door. He said to my father, "Hey Des, man what is happening?"

"Tony's box of marbles finally fell," said he. "I was warning all the time this would happen, but nobody was listening."

"Ah, don't worry too much about it," said Lancelot, going inside again, "more important things in life." He always said this. Whenever something bad happened, he said this to make things cheerful. I wondered if he really meant it or if it was just a way of talking. Like Mr. Lalvani the Punjabi. And nine running.

I slipped past my parents who were blocking the doorway, and started to follow the marbles down the stairs. But the staircase was dark. My father yelled out, "Tony, stop! You'll break you head!" Those steps were really dangerous. I leaned over the railing, and could tell by the sound that the marbles had just reached the passage downstairs. They were now zig-zagging through the wooden poles and beams that supported the broken ceiling.

Then they must have rolled down the front steps and out into the dust of the pavement because they were silent all of a sudden.

We went inside, and my father said, "Enough has happened. All the marble boxes will have to go. You decide how. Give them to your friends, sell them, burn them, anything. But after one week I don't want to see any marbles in the house."

That night I lay in bed thinking of the lost marbles. When everyone was asleep, I got up and went to the balcony. I walked on tiptoe past all the beds. Alice had rolled hers out from under mine, and she was snoring under her blanket. Edwin was on the sofa-cum-bed that creaked loudly every time he turned. My parents would never understand what the marbles meant to me. When they were all gone, I would have to find some other way to spend the time in the evenings.

I looked out in the night. The street was dark and quiet. The building across the road was dark, too, except for one window. Someone was moving behind the curtain, but I could not tell what they were doing. In a few moments that window also went black. I looked at the sky. There were no stars in it. Sometimes, when my father came back from drinking *feni* with Lancelot Braganza, he would be in a good mood. It was strange how the same stuff could make good moods and bad moods. His mouth would smell but his voice would be soft and kind and he would not yell at anyone. Once, he had sat with me on the balcony and said that when he was a little boy, there was never a night which was not brilliant with stars. His father (your grandfather, he explained) would sit with him, like we were sitting, and they would look at the sky, and Grandfather would point out Venus and Jupiter. Now everything had changed, said my father, and the stars and planets were so disgusted with the way life was in Bombay, they had disappeared from the sky, and he did not blame them, he would disappear too if he could. His voice was shaking, and it was very sad. It made me feel funny, but luckily his voice stopped shaking.

Remembering that, I looked down at the pavement. I thought I must be dreaming, because it was shining and sparkling as if covered with a million stars. I rubbed my eyes, then looked again. It was still sparkling, like a tray of jewellery in the window of Vithaldas Jewellers. I used to pass that shop on my way to school everyday.

I wanted to wake my parents so they could look too at how the ruined pavement had changed. It was so wonderful. Then I thought it better to wait till the moring.

I stood there for a long, long time, and don't remember going to bed. I don't remember falling asleep either. Maybe I fell asleep standing at the balcony railing and then walked in my sleep to the bed.

In the morning I told them about the pavement. But I

was too excited, so I don't think I described it properly. And anyway, to describe something so wonderful was difficult.

My father said, "Rubbish. I agree it was beautiful once, before the crooks stole it. Only way it can be wonderful again is if the finely fitted polished slabs come back." Then, "Your son is going crazy, or he had a nice dream," he added to my mother, as if I was not there.

But I insisted it was true, so they went to the window. Only a few jagged gleams from the bits of broken glass came now and then through the dusty stones and pebbles. I was puzzled. Then the sun went behind a cloud, and there was nothing.

"Imagination, a boy's imagination," said my father. "I'm not saying that is a bad thing. But it is good to know it for what it is. And it is still one week for all the marble boxes to go, that has not changed."

He put on his solar hat, picked up his black briefcase, checking inside it, and left to tune pianos. I said to my mother, "I wasn't dreaming, I really saw it. I think you have to wait for the darkness."

She promised that that night she would bring him to the window to look at the pavement.

In the evening, when dusk fell and the street had quieted, I emptied another box of marbles onto the pavement.

Later, when I was in my pyjamas, waiting for all the buildings on the street to go to sleep, my parents came.

"Okay, now where is that wonderful pavement?" said my father, willing to humour me. The hard lines that the *feni* caused to grow downward from the corners of his mouth were not there.

We went to the balcony. But there was nothing. He turned to my mother with a what-did-I-say look. I said,

"You have to wait for a few more minutes."

She squeezed his hand to make him go along with it. She thought I didn't see that. We kept looking at the pavement three storeys below.

It started to happen. A few twinkles first, then some more, and finally the whole pavement was sparkling as if covered with diamonds. It was shining and glittering in the darkness with a beauty that was, as my father said later, otherworldly.

Then the scene started to fade. We looked up. The moon was disappearing behind a cloud. I turned to my parents, and their eyes were shining. Mine must have been, too, because of the way they were looking at me.

"Yes," said my father, with something in his throat, "it's beautiful." He put his arms around me and my mother, then we waited for the moon to reappear. When it sailed out in the open, the stars began to twinkle again in the pavement.

"Go quick," said my father, "call your brother and sister."

I ran to get Edwin and Alice from their beds. The sofa-cum-bed made a loud groan as he got up. Alice came with her blanket over her shoulders. My mother always said the girl was crazy, using it all of the year's three hundred and sixty-five days, even the hot season. They both came grumbling, wondering what their father was up to now. Then they looked, and were not sleepy anymore.

Each time the moon went behind a cloud, we waited patiently for it to emerge. When it was close to time for the moon to set and the sun to rise, and we could no longer keep our eyes open, we went to bed. It was almost morning and we could not sleep too long, but we did not feel exhausted.

The school's annual Prize Distribution Day was to be held on that Friday. Brand new books were given as prizes. Edwin had won many when he was in school. They were still in the showcase with glass doors, alongside the good coffee set we had never used and the glass hen whose top you could lift and the bottom was a bowl in which my mother kept her sewing things. The brand new books had a nice smell. The function always took place on the school's playground, where chairs were placed for the parents and guests. I decided to do the same thing for the playground that had happened to the pavement. That would get rid of the marbles, like my father wanted me to, and give the Prize Distribution a beauty that was otherworldly.

On Friday, I packed my school bag with the remaining boxes of marbles. To get them all in, I had to leave behind some of my books. If the teacher had discovered this, I would have been done for. But as long as I had some open textbook on my desk and pretended to pay attention, she did not bother me.

When all the periods were over, we went down the stairs. Father Lopez stood at the bottom with his feather duster. His hands were behind his back, and the feather duster kept twitching, you could see it as it came and went behind his cassock. He liked the boys to come down in a straight line. Then I went to the bathroom. A few minutes had to pass before I could sneak back up. Once, my marble friend, Dilip, had returned to class after the last bell because he had forgotten something in his desk. The Science master and the English teacher were inside. They were rubbing against each other, and his hands were on her bum. They said nothing, and Dilip left without taking what he had come for. His life was a misery ever after during English and Science, and I did not want this to happen to me.

But on Prize Distribution Day no-one stayed around too long. Teachers wanted to go home, get ready and come back looking *chickna* for the function. The corridor outside my classroom was empty. I took out the boxes from my bag and began turning them over outside the window, careful to keep my head inside. I also looked over my shoulder now and then. First the coloured ones went, then the sodas. It was like emptying a bottle of sodawater. My father used to send me to buy sodawater at the Irani restaurant. He preferred Rogers Soda, but if that was out of stock I had to buy Duke's. He used to mix it in the *feni*. But he also drank sodawater by itself when he had a gas problem. Sometimes he stayed awake all night because of it.

After four boxes were empty, there was a peculiar sound. Like rain falling on a tin roof. That was strange. There should be no sound if the marbles were landing on the dirt surface of the playground. I continued, and so did the noise. Then there were some voices shouting; one sounded like Father Lopez's.

I looked out slowly, a little scared, and at once knew what was going on. My timing was unlucky. The school's six buses had their garages at one end of the playground. They were loaded and leaving when I began to empty the marbles. The noise sounding like rain on tin roofs to me was like thunder to the occupants. Some of the marbles crashed into the windshields and windows. The boys told me later that they rode home in buses with stars that gleamed in sunlight, and when they looked out at streets, all the buildings and cars and people looked broken and disjointed. It was a lot of fun, they said. One thing was sure, my marbles were changing the way things looked, wherever I threw them.

But when I heard Father Lopez's voice, I had to run.

One box of marbles remained. I stuffed it back in my bag and ran downstairs to the school's front gate, while Father Lopez was busy at the back. I hoped he would be pleased later, at night, when he saw how beautiful the playground looked.

The function started at 6.30, and it was still light. I waited for the sky to darken. Then the moon would appear and make the playground as heavenly as my pavement. I didn't tell my parents anything, I wanted it to be a surprise.

But after darkness came, there was no change. Instead, Father Lopez made a special speech: "Today, we might have been in the midst of a calamity instead of celebrating our annual Prize Distribution Day. Today, after school, some irresponsible student threw thousands of marbles from a window upstairs onto this playground and gravely damaged our fleet of school buses. But apart from the damage, imagine, dear parents, the consequences if the situation had not been remedied in time. Imagine, if you will, so many of us slipping and sliding on the marbles, and falling and sustaining all manner of injuries. But thanks to my gallant crew: the *mali* and the sweepers and every available hand, including the teachers who had not yet left, the day was saved. They scoured the playground for the scattered marbles. They made the playground safe again for you, for your children and for our annual Prize Distribution Day. And we all thank them from the bottom of our hearts." There was a lot of clapping.

When I tried very hard, I was able to see a few far-flung sparkles, the ones missed by Father Lopez's gallant cleaning crew, but only because I knew what to look for. No-one else could have noticed them.

Feeling very disappointed, I went home with my parents. My father said, "I hope that at least one time before you finish school you will go up on that stage. Every year Edwin used to win something. He has some silly ideas now, wanting to change from Science to Arts. But in school he was a top student. For General Science or Algebra or something. Always at least one prize."

I was quiet. My mother said, "He will study harder now. You will no, Tony? Once the marbles are all gone, you will do it."

"Can we stand on the balcony tonight?" I asked her.

"We'll see," said my father. "Your mother and I are very tired. If we feel better later, maybe."

I emptied the last box outside the window. If the others did not want to, I would stand alone and watch the pavement.

When it was late at night and I was the only one awake, I went to the balcony. I wished my parents and brother and sister were with me to share it. How could they have seen it once and then not wanted to see it again?

While I wondered, my parents came in. My father said, pretending to be annoyed, "Some bright bloody light is shining in the window, woke me up. No rest even when I'm so tired."

But as we watched, all his tiredness left him. I could tell by the way he was standing and the way his head and shoulders were that he was feeling strong again. Then he said, "This is so wonderful, it feels like there is beautiful singing somewhere inside, in my head or something."

My mother said, "Yes, I am feeling the same way."

Soon Edwin and Alice came. They said that it sounded as if someone was playing music in the quiet night and the sound had woken them up. They came to the window and began watching with us.

Many hours later when the moonlight became faint, we

went to bed, tired and yet feeling fresh. This was the part that made me wonder the most. As if we had not really been standing at the window but sleeping peacefully and dreaming about it.

And when we woke up, no-one talked about it, there was no need to. In the evening, my mother came home from the export company and said that overtime was back to normal, no restrictions, and my father said he had good news too, lots of tuning appointments were booked for him in the coming weeks. That night we stood again on the balcony.

Almost a month after I had dropped the first box of marbles, the pavement began to change. It did not sparkle like it used to, even though the moon was now almost full again. There were large gaps where it remained dark, places where only a few scattered gleams could be seen.

Next morning I went downstairs early, before anyone was up. Outside, a man was scavenging, and I realized what had happened to the pavement.

I wanted to speak to the man, and beg him to leave the remaining marbles in the rubble. But he looked at me so threateningly that I changed my mind. His clothes were torn and he had a dirty beard that had things sticking in it. His nails were long and black and curling. They must not have been cut for years. When my mother cut my nails, she wrapped them in a piece of paper and got rid of them very secretly. She said that if someone found them, they could use them for black magic and do evil to the person from whose fingers the nails came.

That man looked so scary with his long nails that I did not say anything to him. I just returned upstairs quietly.

That night, we gathered on the balcony for the last time. After staring at the pavement, which was now just a broken, sorry surface like before, we went to bed, feeling very tired.

In the morning, for the first time we began to talk about the pavement. We began to talk of what we had lost, of the beauty that shone in the dark, and of the magical way it would start to sparkle when the moon edged out from behind a cloud. and how gradually the whole pavement would be lit as if with a thousand tiny twinkling lights. First my father described it, and then my mother had her turn, and then Edwin, Alice and me.

Although we spoke of the same thing, each of us described it differently, with our own words, and we enjoyed listening to what each one had to say. We also talked about how wonderful we would feel at the end when we finally went to bed, how we felt strength and joy, and now we would not have that anymore.

But a strange thing was happening.

As we talked about it and remembered it all, the same gladness came back to our hearts, and our spirits were uplifted, even more greatly than when we had actually stood before the window. This happened from now on, every time, when we sat and talked about the pavement.

# Vermont

## Debbie Howlett

On the way home, coming back from the movie theatre in the mall on 41st Avenue, the car stalls somewhere near Granville Street. The motor quits and we coast. You turn the engine over, but nothing happens. It doesn't gag, or cough, or sputter to life, it simply *clicks.* I reach out and put my hand on your thigh. Through your jeans I can feel the outline of your empty left front pocket, and I realize that I've never known how far down the pockets in a pair of Levis hang. I mark the inches with a baby finger bent at the knuckle that I've determined to be an exact inch and think again how nice it is to never have to be without an inch. When the four inches strike me as really short, I measure the distance again, my finger blindly tapping along your thigh, while you turn over the engine, *click,* and curse.

We coast until the road starts curving up and the car starts rolling down.

"Stop measuring things!" you yell at me, suddenly jamming the car into P and getting out the driver's side. The door slams shut and everything seems very quiet all of a sudden.

With my scarf, I clear off a portion of the condensation that formed in the parking garage under the mall and watch you make your way around to the front of the car. You fiddle with something about two inches under the hood, and for a minute the expression on your face is one of great anxiety. You pull open the hood and prop it up and I can't see you anymore. Sitting there, I blow on my hands and imagine we've broken down on a deserted stretch of road in the middle of Vermont or somewhere next to a cozy motel with an ice machine and free colour TV. And when you can't get the car going you open the passenger door, hold out your hand, and say something like, *Looks like we have to spend the night, honey.* And *honey* sounds sweet and deep and sincere in the cool Vermont air.

But then you rap on the windshield and accidentally hit your knuckle on the windshield wiper and you curse and shake your hand and it reminds me of the time you burnt your hand on my iron after I told you to iron your own goddammed shirt. Then I'm back from Vermont and I'm in Vancouver and the car is dead on an incline in the middle of 41st Avenue and the parking-brake hasn't worked since June.

"Are you merely going to sit there?" you shout through the windshield, your face taking up the entire space I've just cleared for myself. For a moment, I look out at you, turning the word *merely* over and over in my mind, making it sound like *honey.* Soon your *Are you merely going to sit there?* becomes my *Are you, honey, going to sit there?* I open the door and gingerly step out onto the slick, black road. A star shines high up in the sky. On your side of the car, a station-wagon with a bumper sticker that says I'D RATHER BE SAIL-ING swerves to avoid you and when you wave apologetically at the driver, he honks his horn twice and the baby in the car seat facing backwards gives you the finger.

"Fuck you, Buddy!" you say, and I say that I don't remember Michael Douglas saying anything that sounded remotely like that in the movie.

"Look," you say, so I squint in the dark but that's not what you mean. "Would you please just stand still and hold the flashlight steady?" Your voice borders on testy. I nod and stand in the shadow your back makes holding the flashlight over your shoulder, measuring the distance between us.

I'm standing still and silent beside you, holding the light steady, until a single thread from my scarf starts tickling the inside of my nose. The light flashes into your eyes, then up your nose, then back under the hood, and the car slowly starts to roll down the hill.

A man and his dog come out of a house somewhere on 41st and a door bangs shut. He sees me and smiles, so I wave. Then he sees you, and he can't ignore you chasing and cursing after your car.

"Here," he says, handing me a leash that reminds me of the chain-link Frost fence surrounding our yard I was told not to lick as a child. "He's a nice dog," the man says, sprinting after you. "Big, but nice."

I stand there in the middle of the road saying quiet things like hello there to the dog, watching the two of you chase after the car, when the nice dog places his nose in my crotch and sighs. It tickles at first, but then I can feel the damp imprint his nose leaves on my pants, and it's only cold and uncomfortable.

You and the man who shouts out that his name's Buck manage to slow the car down, but it still rolls a little. I feel awkward and helpless with Buck's dog's nose firmly between my legs, so I try saying dog things like sit pretty and heel and stay and lie down but when nothing seems to work I decide that maybe Buck's dog is deaf. I consider a few hand signals that the dog might know, but give up when I realize that the dog probably can't see anything except the folds my pants make when they're bunched up at the crotch.

When you and Buck reach the top of the hill, you're both out of breath and sweaty. Buck says something about not going anywhere tonight and you agree and start talking about distributor caps and solenoid switches and Die Hard batteries and the next thing you know, we're sitting around the television in Buck's family-room, drinking rum-and-cokes and watching *The Tonight Show* with David Brenner sitting in for Johnny. I remark that I wish they'd let Ed do it sometimes and Buck says that he and I must be a lot alike because he's been thinking along those same lines for some time now.

Buck's wife is the only one drinking straight rum, and I watch her delicately tip back her sherry glass, sip and sigh. And I don't know how pleased she is when Buck suggests we spend the night, but I do notice her lips staying at the sherry glass for what seems like a long time.

"Oh Buck, we couldn't impose," you say and I'm quick to shake my head and agree. When the dog sees me doing this, he leaps into my lap, circles it once, then settles down. Buck says something like, "Down, Roger," but Roger doesn't move.

"We insist, kids," Buck says, looking over at his wife. "Right, Dear?" When he invited us inside, and we were still standing in the porch, Buck told us quietly that his wife's name really is Dear, but it's probably short for something.

"Shore," she says.

"No," I say, "we can catch a bus on Granville Street no problem."

"Not at this hour, honey-bunny," Buck says, referring to his digital wristwatch that has already beeped twice since we've been here.

You smile at me from the Lazy Boy you've settled into, and for the first time since we arrived I notice your hand toying with the mahogany lever on the side. Next to it, there is a leather pocket with this week's *TV Times* and a tattered copy of *The Great Big Crossword Puzzle Book* in it. I wonder how long it will be before you swing back the lever and launch yourself into a reclining position. You look comfortable and right at home among Buck and Dear's black velvet wall hangings and Playboy Club beer mugs and miscellaneous volumes of the *Encyclopaedia Brittanica.* I sip my drink, watching you carefully, and realize that the coke part of my rum-and-coke has gone flat.

"We could take a cab," I say, but Buck tells me not to be silly and don't be shy.

"We got plentya room," Buck says. "Besides, it'll be fun. Tomorrow's Saturday, we can all have…what's it called again that cross between breakfast and lunch?"

"Brunch!" you shout, swinging the lever back and startling Dear a little. She swallows the rest of her rum in one gulp without meaning to and coughs.

"Brunch. That's it. Right, Dear?" His wife says shore again, and turns up the corners of her mouth in what might be a smile, so I smile back at her. She begins to cry, and I don't know if it's your fault or mine.

"Dear?" Buck says. You say something that sounds like ho, ho, and I cross and uncross my legs and arms a few times. Dear gets up and makes for the stairs we came down earlier.

"Are you all right, Dear?" Buck calls out to her.

"Shore," she says, heading up the stairs without a second glance.

You say, "Is she…"

"Don't pay any attention to her. Dear's having a rough time of it," Buck says quietly.

You lean forward and the green leather you're sitting on squeaks and makes a funny sound. Buck leans forward too, and you speak to each other in hushed voices like you're sharing an important secret.

"It's what I told you. It's Dutch," he says, and you nod your head sympathetically. I feel left out, wondering what went on at the bottom of the hill, until sees me looking at him and explains that Dutch is their son.

"He disappeared," Buck whispers. "Late one night on a deserted road outside Moose Jaw, he disappeared just like that." He snaps his fingers. "The police found his truck by the side of the road the next day, but Dutch was gone. Roger and the hogs were there, but Dutch was gone."

On television, David Brenner tells a joke that falls flat and David and Ed look at each other awkwardly and you and I look at David and Ed. Buck looks toward the stairs.

"It's like he drove right into one of those Bermuda tri-

126

angles," he says suddenly.

When Doc strikes up the orchestra, *The Tonight Show* theme song comes on, and Buck switches off the set from a panel of colour-coded controls near his left hand.

"That thing you're setting on folds out into a couch," he says to me. "It's all made up. That's where Dutch used to sleep when he came through town." You smile and thank Buck. I say thanks, too.

"Boy, Rog certainly seems to like you," Buck says, pulling himself up and pointing to the dog in my lap. "Maybe he should sleep down here with you." I ask Buck if he's serious. He laughs and says, "Maybe not." Then, "Come on, Rog." Roger doesn't budge though, not with me pushing from behind or you pulling from in front. And I can't get up because Rog has cut off the circulation in my legs and they've fallen asleep. So I say never mind, Roger can sleep with me. And you.

"Do you play bridge?" Buck asks on his way upstairs. I can only make out his feet on the stairs when he asks us.

I say no and you say a little at the same time. Buck's red plaid slippers suddenly stop and he seems to consider this as he shifts his weight from one foot to the other.

"That's great. I guess," he says, and then, "'night, kids."

With a switch at the top of the stairs, Buck plunges us into darkness. And now the only light in the room comes from the red-and-white Molson Canadian clock over the bar. It hums a little and gives off a strange reddish light that makes me think about shipwrecks and sailor's warnings. You say something about the kindness of strangers and I feel sad wondering whatever happened to Dutch. Then you offer to pull out the couch with me and Roger still on it. I say okay and be careful, and when the couch is horizontal, Roger falls of my lap and hits the floor with a *thud*, but doesn't wake up. The bed folds out over him, but I make sure a bed leg hasn't gored him before we sit down. In the couch, we find one of Roger's bones hidden between the cushions and before I slip under the covers I put Roger's bone beside him in case he wants it when he wakes up. When I look at him, his body starts to tremble a little, so I tell you to come here and have a look. You sprawl out across the bed and hang your head over the side.

"What's the matter with him?" I ask softly because I don't want him to wake up and climb back on top of me.

"It's just a dream," you say and roll back. I ask you what you suppose Roger dreams about, but you don't answer.

"Cats? Do you suppose he dreams about cats?" You say no, you don't suppose he dreams about cats.

"What do you dream about?" you ask me. I shrug my shoulders and start measuring the arm of the couch with my inch.

"You, I guess," I say.

"Measuring," you say. "You dream about measuring."

"I do not," I say. "I dream about you."

"He's probably dreaming about other dogs then," you say as if my answer has somehow helped you come up with yours.

Upstairs, someone's footsteps cross the floor, stop, and then cross back. Then they cross again, stop, and cross back. This goes on for a while, but I can't decide if the footsteps belong to Buck or Dear. They sound too heavy to belong to either of them. I reach out under the covers for you, but you've got your back to me already and your arms stretched out in front of you. I roll over and face the Molson clock and I'd really like to hear you tell me you love me. I'd like those words to come out of your mouth as fast as a hiccup or a burp. And I want not to hear you, not clearly anyway, so you have to say them again, slowly, but your voice cracks and I say what, I can't hear you. And when you say them again, an ambulance goes by somewhere outside and the words are muffled by the siren, so I say sorry? Until you finally get so frustrated you shout them at me so loudly Buck or whoever's pacing up there calls down to ask what's up?

But you don't, and I fall asleep to the sound of footsteps crossing the floor above us. In the middle of the night, your hand starts rubbing your favourite part of my back and when I say huh? you tell me I'm snoring again. I apologize saying I'm sorry and tell you I think I caught a cold standing on 41st Avenue holding your flashlight.

# Love in the Time of Cliches

**Diane Schoemperlen**

*...it was love at first sight...*

Shortly after Carmen falls irretrievably in love with Abraham, she notices that she is often at a loss for words. This is unusual for Carmen, who has been told many times that she's been blessed with the gift of the gab. She supposes that she inherited or appropriated this gift from her mother, Maureen. Most of Carmen's childhood memories feature the sound of Maureen's lilting voice running as an undercurrent through everything, the melodious background music to their daily lives.

There, for instance, was Carmen, already a devoutly practising insomniac at an early age, tossing and turning in her narrow bed till the sheets were twisted like seaweed round her ankles. She could hear her mother in the living-room, talking to her father, Frank, who never said much in reply, who was in fact probably stretched out on the couch half-asleep, not even listening, but Maureen didn't seem to notice or mind much. Carmen was on the tip of being a teenager then and often coaxed herself to sleep with fantasies of what it would be like to have a man, a full-grown, not-too-hairy man beside her in the bed, a man who would sleep all night long with his arm around her waist, his hand between her legs, not caressing, just cradling and holding her close, quietly.

It was not until Carmen took on the surly, self-absorbed silence of adolescence that she began to wish Maureen would just SHUT UP. She never had anything important to say anyway, Carmen fumed silently. Especially first thing in the morning, Maureen was just like a magpie: yack, yack, yack. She just loved the sound of her own voice, Carmen thought, and closed her long-suffering eyes while her oatmeal congealed.

It was almost ten years later, long after Carmen had surfaced from beneath the iceberg of adolescence, had finished university, moved away from home and settled into her own eventual adult life, that she understood how her mother's sometimes manic loquaciousness might actually have been compensation for the fact that she *knew* she had nothing important to say or, if she did, for the fact that she was afraid to say it.

Now Carmen finds she can afford to be sympathetic and

doesn't mind admitting that, in terms of volubility anyway, she is her mother's daughter. It is an inheritance that serves Carmen well, both in her teaching job and in her personal life.

She is often admired for her ability to talk to anyone about anything. She can talk to her students about their families (who don't understand them), their boyfriends (who are collectively unco-operative and afraid of commitment), their wardrobes (which must look stylish but not too studied), their hair (which must be easy to take care of and yet look perfect at all times). She can talk to her fellow English teachers about the existential commitment in *Macbeth*, the symbol of the green light in *The Great Gatsby* and the passage of time in the novels of Virginia Woolf. She can even talk to people she doesn't particularly like about things she isn't the least bit interested in. She talks to the jocks about football, to the math teachers about sine, cosine and tangent, to the cashier in the cafeteria about the occupational hazard of breaking your fingernails on the cash-register drawer and to the foreign students about the price of tea in China. She is seldom stuck for a snappy answer to anything.

She works hard during the week and goes to lots of parties on weekends. Usually the first to arrive and the last to leave, she can dance and dance and never get tired, drink and drink and never pass out or throw up. She is the legendary life of the party. Her friends marvel at her stamina, her energy, her irrepressible love of life. She is, someone once said admiringly, the kind of person you cannot ever imagine asleep.

They don't know the half of it. They don't know about the insomnia, Carmen waking up in a sweat (hot or color or an indescribable combination of both) at 3.14 AM, her heart pounding so hard she can see it trembling beneath her nightgown, and then she can't go back to sleep even though she has to get up for work at 6.30, so she lies there worrying about anything and everything that crosses her mind, watching the red numbers on the digital clock click inexorably over until morning.

Her friends don't know how she sits by herself for hours on end not doing anything, not listening to music or looking out the window or anything, but just sitting there, brooding and stewing and travelling further and further inside herself, trying to catch a glimpse of what is really in there.

They don't know how she often plays a game with herself when walking down the street: looking closely at total strangers and trying to imagine them making love—not necessarily to her, but to anyone. That woman there in the purple shorts, the one with the snotty-nosed toddler on a leash and the prune-faced baby screaming in the stroller. That man there in the three-piece suit with his neck bulging over his perfectly knotted tie, his hair combed forward over his bald spot, a chunky gold wedding-band on his third left finger. Could they ever really have been laughing and snuggling, naked and happy in their lovers' arms? There are, Carmen has discovered, a great many people who, despite all evidence to the contrary, cannot be imagined into love in any position. She is afraid that she has become one of them.

Carmen has had lovers, of course—lots of them, in fact. Too many lovers, some people (her mother) might say. But nothing has ever worked out. With the twenty / twenty hindsight acquired somewhere around her thirtieth birthday, Carmen can see these men now as a long and relatively listless line of losers. Not one of them, she sees now, could have changed her life even if she'd wanted them to. Once, in a fit of foolishness precipitated by a six-month dry spell and a bottle of wine, she sat down to make a list of them (in order of appearance, not importance). When she got halfway through, when she got to the veterinarian who, in his exuberance to get her into his waterbed, knocked over the hamster cage on the nightstand, killing the stupid smelly little thing, when she discovered that she couldn't even remember his name (Kevin? Karl? Keith?), she was so appalled and depressed that she went to bed, where, of course, she couldn't sleep for a long time anyway and then all of her dreams were dotted with furry little dead things.

Her friend, Lorraine, a woman with a similarly chequered and disappointing past, once sent Carmen a cute card that said: "A question every woman asks herself...Is it possible that I deserve the kind of men I attract?" So Carmen smiled wryly, said, "Yes, well, yes," and kept on wondering, kept on trying to convince herself that none of it mattered anyway, that she preferred to be alone anyway, that sex wasn't what it was cracked up to be anyway, was definitely not one of the basic human needs like food, water and shelter. And what was all the fuss about anyway when there were so many more important things to be considered?

And sometimes she even manages to look fondly forward to spending the rest of her life alone. Sometimes, when she can embrace it from just the right angle, she is able to conjure an image of herself as very tall, very thin, standing very straight, wearing something white and willowy, feeling stoic and serene, untouched by human hands and so, unsullied, uncomplicated and clean.

Carmen's friends misinterpret her liveliness as the result of a natural ebullient energy, when really it is the result of a persistent low-grade anxiety that escalates according to the situation at hand. Knowing that she has a party to go to on Friday night is enough to keep her going all week long. By Friday morning she is so keyed-up that all day at work she is thinking of it: of what she will wear (does she need a new shirt? a black one? new pants? a new hairdo?), of what she will say (did she tell that story about the hamster last week or what about the guy who told her she was pretty well-preserved for her age and then couldn't understand why she dumped him?), of what she will drink (beer makes her sloppy but affectionate and gregarious, Scotch leaves her lucid but brave), of who else might be there, of the music, the dancing, the sky going dark outside the windows and then maybe coming light again too, pinkish and pale, and she won't have to sleep (or try to) all night long.

Nobody knows that she is the first to arrive because, by that time, she can't take the anticipation a minute longer and has to swing into action before she explodes. And that she is the last to leave because, by that time, she can't bear to admit that the party is over and nothing has happened. (She is never quite sure what she is expecting to happen but she *is* sure that if it ever does, she'll know. This is akin to what her mother told her years ago when Carmen asked her how you know when you're really in love, and Maureen said, mysteriously, maddeningly, as all mothers do, "Oh, you'll know, you'll just *know*."

So it is at a party, naturally enough, that Carmen first meets Abraham. A party thrown for no good reason other than that they are all mired in the backwater of mid-February and they just need to let loose. Carmen is wearing her tightest black jeans, her baggy hot-pink sweatshirt and silver hoop earrings the size of saucers. Her hair, for once, has turned out just right and her black leather jacket, she thinks, adds just the right hint or promise of danger.

She has never seen Abraham before in her life (he is new in town, working in the English Department at the university, so she's been told) but as she watches him browsing through the tape collection, selecting one and then plugging it into the machine, she suddenly thinks, Now there's a man I'd like to have around all the time.

For about a minute and a half the fact that he has chosen her own favourite tape seems merely coincidental. Emmylou Harris sings, *I would walk all the way / From Boulder to Birmingham / If I thought I could see / I could see your face.*

When Abraham asks Carmen to dance and takes her in his arms, it all makes perfect and sudden sense.

*...love makes the world go round...*

It is exactly two weeks later that Carmen notices she is more and more often at a loss for words. Her friends are concerned at first. They think she is depressed. When they realize that she is just in love, they take to teasing her gently while she smiles stupidly (they call it "mooning") with the realization that Abraham is the only person in the whole world she wants to talk or listen to anyway. Sometimes her friends complain that she's just no fun anymore.

She can feel herself beginning to shed the cynicism with which she has protected herself for years. It comes peeling off her in ragged sheets like sunburned skin. Sometimes it is embarrasssing, like when she does get talkative and catches herself quite unconscionably running off at the mouth about a beautiful sunset, a perfect tree or the precious light of a misty morning. Her friends take to rolling their eyes impatiently whenever she begins to wax poetic about how WONDERFUL everything is. They don't understand how loving Abraham is like getting new glasses that amplify and intensify everything so that even the colour of the clouds, the sound of the rain and the taste of her chicken-salad sandwich at lunch are magnificent and miraculous.

Abraham usually picks Carmen up after work and, as they drive through the familiar city streets, they joyfully point out landmarks and points of interest to each other. There is their favourite house on the corner of Dundas and Tait, the vine-covered brick one with the verandah, the dormers, the bay window through which they can see a stone fireplace, floor-to-ceiling bookshelves and hanging plants everywhere. They are both thinking, Someday we'll have a house like that. Even though they see it every day, it never ceases to amaze them.

They comment happily on sleepy cats curled on porches or window ledges, frisky black squirrels, bright-eyed and bushy-tailed, chasing each other from branch to branch, rosy-cheeked children in pink snowsuits and bunny hats, plump lumpy snowmen with carrot noses and corn-cob pipes. The whole neighbourhood strikes them as happy and handsome, resplendent and promising, tangible proof of the power of love.

When they see a young couple kissing on the corner, the girl's face tilting up to meet the boy's lips, her naked throat an offering, tantalizing with trust, Carmen and Abraham feel tender and empowered and Carmen lays her head on his shoulder while they wait for the light to change and the boy on the corner buries his face in the girl's cold hair.

On Fridays they stop at The Brunswick Bar for a drink on the way home. At The Brunswick they hold hands across the table and share a plate of nachos with cheese.

One Friday afternoon in the car when both of them are singing along with the Top 40 AM radio love songs (*I had the time of my life / And I owe it all to you*), they notice that, much as this music used to seem sappy and naïve, it has lately become poignant and perceptive.

Suddenly they simultaneously realize that most of what has been coming out of their mouths these days is one massive love-soaked starry-eyed cliché.

They go directly to The Brunswick to talk it over. The bar, as usual on Friday afternoon, is crowded with other hard-working people celebrating the end of another busy week. Everyone feels exuberant: they're buying drinks for each other as fast as they can, laughing uproariously, taking off their jackets and ties, letting their hair down for a few happy hours. Abraham and Carmen are lucky enough to get their favourite table and they smile and nod at familiar faces as they make their way to the back corner by the window. It's a cold dark day with snow clouds piled like blankets in the northern sky. The fireplace is lit and the room closes cosily in around the orange-tinted light, the smell of wood smoke, the sound of jazz jusic.

They are disgruntled at first by their unsettling revelation. They have always thought of themselves as creative, original, sophisticated and very amusing people. They look cautiously around The Brunswick wondering if anyone has noticed the change in them but been too polite to mention it. Today they consciously resist the urge to feed nachos to each other.

No wonder they can only talk to each other these days! How could they say such things to their friends, to their conscientious politically-correct friends who are all wrapped up in the larger issues: the environment, the Third World, the nuclear arms race, poverty, pornography, abortion, AIDS and injustice. Certainly their friends have their love lives too, but they seem to look upon these liaisons with practical, matter-of-fact eyes. They are careful never to neglect their work, their other friends, or their social consciences in favour of their loves and / or their lusts. They are mature, independent, self-sufficient, self-controlled, meticulously realistic people who would never let love get in the way of anything.

Before she fell in love with Abraham, Carmen was just like them. Not since one misguided juvenile moment in Grade 10 has she turned down an evening with her female friends in favour of staying home and waiting for the phone to ring. She once laughed out loud at a woman who kept a snapshot of her lover on the dashboard of her car when he was away travelling and thought it probably served this woman right when she ran out of gas because the picture was over the gas gauge. She used to sneer churlishly at couples who kissed on corners. She had, a scant six weeks ago, turned down a date with a man she had been interested in for ages because he invited her to go and see a band called The High Heels whose lyrics were notoriously sexist and, besides, there was a rally that same night for animal rights.

Abraham too admits that he once broke a hot date with a gorgeous lustful woman because he wanted to stay home and reread *Madame Bovary*. And that he had once ended a fairly serious relationship with a woman named Wanda because she said nuclear war was inevitable so what was the point in getting all worked up about it?

Now Carmen and Abraham, by comparison both to their friends and to their former selves, are either iconoclastic or insipid lovebirds.

They order more beer and consider the nature of clichés.

Carmen recalls an incident from a Grade 11 English class

when, in a short essay on Dickens' *Great Expectations,* she used the phrase "the eyes are the windows of the soul" and referred to it as "that old cliché." Her teacher, Miss Crocker, had put a question mark in the margin and a comment saying she'd never heard that saying before. Even then Carmen was aghast and never trusted Miss Crocker again.

Abraham suggests that the reason clichés become clichés in the first place is because they are true and that's why they come so easily to mind. "So yes," he says, "there must be a great many people in the world who have skin white as snow, hair black as night, lips red as cherries, voices clear as bells and eyes just like diamonds or stars."

Carmen frowns into her half-empty glass.

Abraham elaborates on his theory: "Certainly, all over the world there must be thousands, if not millions, of people who are smart as whips, quick as winks, busy as bees—"

Carmen catches the spirit and they trade clichés across the table like playing cards:

"—right as rain," she offers. "Nervous as cats, quiet as mice, happy as clams—"

"—wicked as witches, thick as bricks, crazy as loons, strong as bulls, big as houses—"

"—mad as hatters, sick as dogs, cold as ice—"

"—wise as owls, bald as billiard balls, weak as kittens, naked as jaybirds—"

"—hot as blazes—"

"—nutty as fruitcakes—"

"—slow as molasses in January-"

"—pretty as pictures—"

"—ugly as sin—"

"—as old as the hills."

"So what's wrong with that?" asks Abraham.

"And drunk as skunks too," Carmen adds, taking another sip. She is not quite convinced that clichés might actually be acceptable currency in intelligent conversation. "When was the last time you saw a drunk skunk?" she counters skeptically. She also points out that people who sleep like babies have obviously never had one. And those who insist they are happy as larks know next to nothing about the real secret lives of birds, about the pressures they're under, trying to get that nest built out of thin air, laying those eggs and then sitting on them for God knows how long, hatching the babies, feeding them, teaching them how to fly—and having to keep on singing the whole time too.

"But what about love?" Abraham asks. "What about 'I love you?' What about 'I love you like there's no tomorrow?'"

Their sheepish chagrin is replaced quickly enough by an amused relief at finding themselves finally able to indulge their nascent romanticism, a tendency they had convinced themselves was a shameful weakness to be forever monitored, suppressed and camouflaged for their higher-minded friends, indeed for the entire modern world. They marvel now at their ability to say romantic things to each other without feeling embarrassed or self-conscious, without having to make fun of themselves for being in love. They congratulate themselves on their new-found ability to say such things over and over again with a straight face and without gagging.

"Next thing you know," Carmen warns, "we'll be reading romance novels. Our hearts will be pounding, our breasts will be heaving, our hands will be quivering. Even the tips of our fingers will be tingling and electrified. We will be throbbing all over the place."

They say to hell with the cynical high-minded modern world. They have been tempted (or trying) to fall in love like this all their lives. They have nothing to hide, they can wear their passion everywhere. They are immaculate lovers, shameless. They will never be ordinary people again.

*...you are always on my mind...*

Abraham is coming over for a special dinner to celebrate their first-month anniversary. Carmen spends the whole day, Saturday, getting ready while Abraham puts in a few hours of work at the university. She gets up early and reads cookbooks. Then she goes downtown to gather the ingredients for the meal, which will be a nourishing feast fit for a king. Abraham is a man who loves to eat and Carmen loves to cook.

At the A&P, Carmen hums along with the muzak (*...the girl from Ipanema goes walking...*) and grins when they play a mutilated instrumental version of "You Light Up My Life." She makes her way slowly up and down the aisles, instead of tearing through the whole store in ten minutes like she usually does. She reads labels and considers prices carefully, instead of grabbing items off the shelves with one hand while still pushing the cart with the other so that it never stops moving. She waits patiently behind an elderly woman who has left her cart blocking the cereal aisle and smiles sympathetically as the woman tries to decide between regular oatmeal and the new quick-cooking kind. (She is not happy to recall the time an innocent but unsteady old man tried to shuffle past her in the produce section and banged into her cart with his and she told him to fuck off.) She lovingly selects the zucchini, the onions, the green peppers, weighs them gently in each hand, caresses them intimately, then lays them down in the cart as if they were alive. She hand-picks the mushrooms from the bulk bin instead of buying a pre-packaged plastic tub. She imagines them slippery and flavourful in Abraham's mouth. She is patient with the cashier who is new on the job and doesn't have the hang of the electronic scanner yet. She loves every minute of it.

On her way into the seafood store, she bumps into her friend, Debbie, from school. Debbie teaches Health. Debbie says she just read an article in *Popular Psychology* that said that over 75% of any given person's thoughts on any given day are about either food or sex. The article also said that the average person has seven sexual fantasies per day.

Carmen thinks, What? Is that all? Only seven?

Debbie says, "I don't believe it. Nobody has that many! I've never had that many. I must be one of those people who fantasize about hot fudge sundaes instead!" She heads for the Dairy Queen, chuckling.

In the seafood store, Carmen buys a whole pound of fresh jumbo shrimp with the shells still on. While the man behind the counter wraps them up, she tells him she's making a special dinner tonight for her lover and they'll just have to see if it's true what they say about seafood being an aphrodisiac. She isn't even embarrassed when the man stares at her as if she's gone straight out of her mind.

At a gift store, she buys two pale blue candles and two white porcelain candle holders. She imagines Abraham's tender face touched by their elegant light. At the flower shop, she buys a bouquet of dusty pink astermaria, arranged with graceful green ferns and white Baby's Breath. She imagines Abraham pressing his face close into them and sighing deeply. At the liquor store, she buys a bottle of brandy. She imagines Abraham lifting the glass to his full moist lips, tasting the wine as thoroughly as he will afterwards taste her nipples and the back of her neck.

She spends the whole afternoon chopping, slicing and dicing, singing along with Emmylou: *I don't want to hear a sad story / Full of heartbreak and desire.* She puts together the zucchini and barley casserole, then the cold lentil salad. She has to consult *The Joy of Cooking* about how to clean the shrimp. The cookbook has instructions and a diagram: "Shelling is easy—a slight tug releases the body shell from the tail. De-vein using a small pointed knife or the end of a toothpick, as sketched. This is essential." In the diagram, two disembodied female hands lay a small black knife upon a plump shrimp that looks like a fat peapod. The procedure may be essential but it's not easy and it takes Carmen a long time to master this tugging and hacking, so that the blue veins come snapping out of the meat like elastic bands. She marinates the shrimp in olive oil, parsley, basil, wine and garlic. There is garlic in everything because they love garlic and the smell of it in the warm kitchen is pungent.

Finally content with her efforts, she sits down to read the newspaper and wait for Abraham. She recognizes that, short of an apron and bare feet, the whole scene is a cliché. *The way to man's heart…*

"The way to a man's heart," she used to like to quip for her friends, "is an unmarked minefield." Or: is a barbed-wire fence, an electric one at that. Is a shot in the dark. Is a roller-coaster ride to hell. At the time she thought she was vastly amusing. Now she feels sorry for her former self.

"Contentment," she used to say, "is for cows."

"Patience," she used to say, "is a virgin."

In the newspaper, she reads the story of two lovers reunited finally and forever after seventeen years and her eyes mist over lightly with sweet warm tears.

And so it is in the power of true love to liberate all emotions unequivocally and without restraint. It is no longer necessary to deny your emotional excesses. No longer necessary to pretend you have something in your eye when you cry at the long-distance commercials on television. No longer necessary to try and convince anyone, not even yourself, that you stopped believing in "happily ever after" around the same time you got smart about Santa Claus and the Easter Bunny. It is no longer necessary to keep your heart in check and your passion under control. You can be as flagrant and ecstatic as you have always wanted to be.

Abraham arrives with more flowers, white wine and a chocolate cheesecake for dessert. They kiss for a long time in the doorway, stranded on the stairs.

"My lover," Carmen says, "my lover." The mere sound of the word lets loose a voluptuous leaping in her heart, her stomach or some hitherto unknown, unexercised internal organ. The other beautiful feast will just have to wait.

*...I can't live if living is without you...*

In the morning they make love again. Carmen is above him, her hands on his shoulders, his tongue licking her breasts, his hands squeezing her buttocks as she moves on him in small circles, his long thin fingers sliding in and out of all her moist places, beads of sweat and her long hair falling into her eyes, into his, and when she comes he says, "I love you, I love you." He says he loves the way she looks right at him when she comes, the way she comes *into* him rather than away, the way she doesn't go off to some other planet where he can no longer reach her. And he is right, she is not transported; rather, she is transformed. In his innocent arms she becomes the person she has always hoped to be.

Everywhere their bodies are like mouths, slippery and warm, brimming with nerve endings and succulent tastebuds.

Abraham holds her there on top of him. She rests her wet face on his wet chest and she can feel his heart beating against her forehead like a pulse in her own brain. When he says, "I want to hold you like this forever," she can feel the words as much as hear them. Even if she were deaf, she would know what he was saying. They stretch out side by side face-down on the big bed and take turns tracing words with their fingertips on each other's bare backs and then trying to guess what they are. They make words like "hope," "love," "forever," "hearts," "sweethearts." Even if they were blind, they would dwell in the language of love.

Abraham says it's his turn to make breakfast. Carmen gets to luxuriate in her own laziness, lolling around in the messy bed, the smell of their love-making still on the sheets, the smell of his hair still on the pillow. While Abraham clatters around in the kitchen, she tries smelling her own skin, her arms, the crook of her elbow, tries to catch that smell of herself that Abraham is always saying he loves so much. Except for a possible hint of garlic from last night's meal still on her hands, she cannot smell anything special. This is akin, she supposes, to not being able to tickle yourself—why can't you? If she sprawls crossways on the bed and leans over the edge, she can just see Abraham in the kitchen at the stove. The sight of him stirring and tasting, bare-chested in his blue jeans, leaves her weak-kneed with pleasure.

She comes into the kitchen in her pink chenille housecoat that makes her feel like an irresistible if slightly dissolute movie queen from the fifties. Dishing up their hot porridge, Abraham tells her that she looks glamorous. The sash of the housecoat comes loose as she sits down at the table. Abraham smiles at her brown nipples, which look like another pair of eyes, blinking with surprise at the light.

"There is," he says, laughing, "a fine line between sordid and glamorous."

Porridge is something that Carmen would never make for herself (if only because it would remind her of those mornings when she was busy hating her mother, Maureen, who was rambling on about the virtues of a hot breakfast while Carmen's oatmeal turned to concrete in her bowl). But cooked up now by Abraham, it is the best thing she has ever eaten. And when he expounds on the virtues of a hot breakfast, she is touched by his loving concern for her health.

From the kitchen window, they watch the empty Sunday morning street. It has rained heavily all night and now the temperature is dropping quickly, freezing the rain as it falls, forming a skin of ice on everything in sight. It is springtime, or it should be. (Carmen thinks again of Maureen who, whenever the weather was unusual, said it was because of those damned Russians out in space always shooting at the moon.) An occasional car slides past the house, windshield wipers flapping ineffectually, ferrying intrepid men in rumpled suits and devout women in subdued hats to worship at the churches of their choice. They laugh, but not unkindly, at the woman from next door making her way down the treacherous sidewalk with a box of salt in her hand, sprinkling it on the ice in front of her as she inches along.

They decide it is a good day to be decadent. They close up all the curtains again, put a little brandy in their coffee, and carry their cups into the living-room. They've got classical music on the stereo, Beethoven's "Ode to Joy": *O friends, no more these sounds! / let us sing more cheerful songs, / more full of joy!*

They're curled up on the chesterfield like luxurious cats and the hanging lamp in the corner drops a circle of yellow light down around them like a tent. They take turns reading poetry to each other.

The day unravels in slow motion around them and they know in their hearts how beautiful they truly are.

By mid-afternoon it is still raining and they are still nestled there in each other's arms. Abraham is dozing and Carmen is suspended somewhere between thinking and dreaming, all of her borders blurred. Now that she has at last learned how to love, she worries sometimes about how much now she has to lose.

As if from a great snow-covered stony height, she feels Abraham's fingers go limp and fall away from hers. Her eyes snap open.

To look into the future and not see them together is like going blind.

In his sleep, Abraham tucks his hand between her legs where it is furry and moist and he sighs.


*...wish you werehere...*


In August, Camen goes home to visit her parents for two weeks. Abraham drives her to the airport where they re-enact the time-honoured scene, hugging and promising while Carmen hides her teary eyes in his neck. At the last minute, Abraham tucks the Emmylou Harris tape into her purse, and says, "Reinforcements."

The small plane gaining altitude after take-off fishtails like a car skidding on the ice in slow motion. Carmen, who does not like flying at the best of times, is praying silently at the top of her lungs, praying to a God she is not sure she believes in but whom she is not averse to invoking when she thinks it might help, praying, Please don't let me die now, not now, not now when I'm in love. But then, sinking back into her seat, she thinks, Oh well, all right then, go ahead, at least I won't have died without learning how to love.

But of course she doesn't die. She smiles gratefully at the calm competent stewardess and tries to enjoy the flight. The man in the seat beside her is headfirst in his briefcase, avoiding her glance, clearly not interested in making conversation. She looks out the window.

The sight of the familiar countryside falling away from her at odd angles as the plane continues to climb is mesmerizing. She is already writing a letter to Abraham in her head. She must remember to tell him about these lakes like the little mirrors on that embroidered Indian bag she used to carry, about these trees like broccoli, too green to be true, about this highway like an artery, these country roads like veins. She relaxes and closes her eyes. The two women in front of her are gossiping in shrill but thrilled voices, using words like "odious," "flagrant," "screaming," and "wild-eyed." Over the drone of the plane, nothing they are saying connects. There is another voice, a pretty voice in her own head, running as the soothing undercurrent through everything. It takes her a minute to realize it is the voice of Emmylou, singing.

As Carmen drifts further away, the voice in her head becomes that of Maureen superimposed upon a picture of Carmen in her sandbox, mucking around with a yellow plastic shovel and a little red pail while her mother leaned against the white picket fence, chatting with the neighbour lady, Mrs. Lutz, who smiled and nodded knowingly as Maureen considered at length the possibilities of the weather, the problems of the old wringer washing-machine (which once got a good grip on her left hand and flattened all four fingers), and what would become of the Watson house now that the Widow Watson had finally passed on, poor old thing? Mrs. Lutz was poking around in her big garden while they talked, handing Maureen vegetables over the fence: waxy green cucumbers, plump red tomatoes, crisp orange carrots with the dirt still on them. Maureen carried them into the house cradled in her apron as if they were alive. Carmen didn't mind being left alone in the yard. Not until she heard the sound of a train on the track at the end of the street and as it bore down on her, she ran the whole length of the yard screaming, banged the screendoor open and flew into her mother's safe arms in the safe yellow kitchen.

Maureen and Frank are waiting at the airport and Carmen is surprised at the lump that rises in her throat when Maureen takes her in her arms. For a minute, Carmen thinks Maureen is wearing little white gloves, wrist-length, the kind she would have been wearing twenty years ago with her white feathered hat with the veil. But no, it's just that Maureen's skin is so white that her hands look disembodied, as if hung from the sleeves of her fancy black blouse. Her father, Frank, pats her gently on the back.

Maureen talks all the way home in the car, while Frank drives smiling, and Carmen marvels, as she does every year, at how nothing and everything has changed: how the street looks the same but wider and the houses look the same too but smaller and cleaner.

Maureen's kitchen hasn't changed either: there is the same flooring (white with gold swirls), the same arborite kitchenette set (blue with black specks), Maureen's collection of little ceramic animals and birds gathered from boxes of Red Rose tea and arranged on the windowsill above the sink, Carmen's Grade 12 school picture still stuck to the fridge with an owl magnet.

But this year, Carmen finds she does not immediately turn back into a seething sixteen-year-old the minute she steps into the house. This time, as she lays her suitcase down on her old bed, she is still a grown woman with a good job. She is still a happy woman with a photograph of Abraham in the gold locket at her throat. It is an antique locket that Maureen gave her when she left home and so it is engraved in delicate curling script with Maureen's initials instead of her own. She has never worn it before and now, with Abraham's picture inside, the locket is a potent talisman that will protect her from all sadness, all evil, despair. Abraham's spirit will not desert her. Whenever the ache of loneliness surges up into her throat so that she can feel it like a second pulse, she rubs the gold locket between her thumb and forefinger until it is warm, warm as his hands on her cheeks when he kisses her closed eyelids, warm as the sound of his voice in the dark.

This time, too, Maureen and Frank seem to sense the change in her and, indeed, they treat her like an adult instead of like a seething sixteen-year-old. She finds she can even afford this time to remember scenes from those tortured adolescent years with a nostalgic fondness for her own plaintive perpetual whining ("Stop treating me like a child!") and for Maureen's condescending triumphant reasoning ("Then stop acting like one!").

She can sit there at the table eating a pressed ham and Kraft processed-cheese sandwich on white bread, drinking Lone Star beer right out of the can, skimming through Frank's *National Enquirer* and Maureen's *True Romances,* listening to Frank suck his teeth while Maureen complains about the new people next door who never mow their grass and what will become of this neighbourhood anyway? She can sit there calmly without hating them at all. She can think with amusement: Ah, the life I left behind!

She can even look at the fake fireplace in the living-room (plaster of Paris painted like bricks, which Maureen was always touching up with a piece of grey chalk when the paint got chipped and there is a revolving orange lightbulb below the metal grate, which is filled with charcoal briquets) without cringing or wishing she could take a sledge-hammer to the damn thing.

She can think of Abraham's face between her naked trembling thighs and she can hear him whispering her name when she comes. For once in her life, she does not feel guilty about anything, least of all about growing up.

And so the lovers, the true lovers, may become at long last generous and genuine, capable of expanding in all directions at once without ever losing track of themselves. All memories are bearable, all dreams are possible, and the future feels like a very fine thing full of truth and spirit and tender power.

On the third day of her visit, Carmen goes to bed early because the time will not pass. She has always had a problem with time. As a child, she was always trying to coax or trick the hours into hurrying up because there was always something she could hardly wait for and Maureen was always warning her, "Girl, you're wishing your life away."

Now she lies awake in the half-dark watching the numbers on the digital clock and listening to the Emmylou Harris tape. She can hear her mother in the kitchen, talking on the phone to her sister, Giselle.

Caremen can picture Maureen perched on the stool by the phone, twirling the coiled cord with one hand and doodling all over the phone book with the other. Maureen and Giselle are having the same conversation they had twenty years ago while Carmen struggled with her math homework and eavesdropped. They would talk on about shopping, cooking, their respective aches and pains, some program they'd both watched on TV and hated or loved.

Often they would reminisce about giving birth: Giselle to her two boys and Maureen to Carmen, who is an only child. Childbirth, Carmen discovered while eavesdropping, is something that mothers never tire of talking about, no matter how many years have by then intervened. They love to tell each other the numbers again and again, slipping them back and forth like the balls on an abacus: hours in labour, hours in the delivery-room, minutes between contractions, how many pushes before the head popped out like a pumpkin. It is a competition of sorts to see who has suffered the most pain and indignity and survived. It is also proof that those who say you won't remember the pain are lying.

Sometimes they talked about their own childhoods and how they hated each other when they were kids: "Do you remember when you broke the teapot over my head? Do you remember when I tried to stick your head down the hole in the outhouse?" It was a wonder they hadn't killed each other. They laughed and laughed and left red lipstick all over their respective receivers. When Maureen hung up, she looked flushed and girlish again.

Tonight, after she hangs up, she taps on Carmen's door and slips into the dark room. "That's pretty music," she says and curls up on the bed with Carmen. She is wearing her chenille housecoat, which falls half-open to reveal a shiny white slip with spaghetti straps and Carmen can see just the top of her mother's breasts, which are beautiful and luminous like the inside of seashells.

They wiggle around on the bed until they are both sitting propped against the headboard with the pillows behind them. Carmen lays her head against her mother's shoulder and tells her all about Abraham. She tells her how he is kind, sensitive, intelligent, funny, warm, wise, healthy, peaceful, passionate, serious, generous, gentle, beautiful and strong. How he is the man she'd almost given up hoping to meet, how he is the man she has had in her heart all along. She shows Maureen his picture in the locket.

Her father seems to have graciously accepted the fact that he can inhabit only the fringes of this moment and she can hear him paddling around in the kitchen in his slippers, humming and making cocoa and toast.

As she talks, Carmen feels like she has been doing this all her life. But the truth is she has not told her mother anything important since the time Mickey Roach kissed her on the mouth at recess and Carmen punched him in the nose.

Years later, there was the time Reg Henderson took her out to the airport parking-lot where all the would-be lovers used to go and she let him touch her small breasts under her sweater and there was a tickling between her legs and she wanted him to touch her there but then she pushed him off her and felt sick to her stomach with loving it and hating it. She was crying when she got home and her hair was a mess and of course Maureen was waiting up for her but when she tried to talk to her, Maureen said, "I don't want to hear about it," and then she went to bed, leaving Carmen alone in the dark living-room, trying to make sense of herself.

Years later still, there was the time Carmen called home long-distance and she was telling Maureen about the trip to Toronto she'd made that weekend with her boyfriend, Terry, and how their hotel room was so elegant, an oak four-poster bed with curtains and everything, and Maureen said, "I don't want to hear about it," and Carmen, in a flash of futile anger said, "What the hell do you think I do out here—knit?" But Maureen was already talking about the new wallpaper they'd hung in the bathroom and Carmen couldn't get another word in edgewise.

Now Carmen tells her mother that Abraham is the best lover she has ever had and Maureen doesn't even flinch. She doesn't laugh or change the subject either. She is silent and then she says, "Yes," and her voice is smiling.

They talk about Abraham for two hours straight and the time passes so slowly that missing him is exquisite.


*I'm so lonesome I could cry...*

Long after Maureen and Frank have gone to bed, Carmen is still awake. Listening to her parents giggling and whispering in bed, it occurs to her for the first time that they are in love, still in love.

When the phone on the night-table rings, it is Abraham.

"I miss you," he says and his voice is rich.

"When you get home," he says, "I want to make love to you until you pass out."

"I've been reading about lions," he says, "who have been known to make love 80 times a day, and this," he says, "is something to strive for."

The sound of his voice in the dark makes her wet.

After Carmen hangs up, she thinks about a summer evening at Black Bridge Falls when they had been swimming, were sitting afterwards on the high grassy bank in their bathing-suits, just watching the river flow. Carmen pushed him gently back onto the grass, pulled down his bathing suit, and took him into her mouth and he moaned and arched up toward her.

In the dark bedroom now, she pretends the cool sheets against her naked body are his skin against hers and she strokes her breasts until the nipples grow hard and she touches herself just the way he touches her and she imagines him watching her as she slides her own fingers in and out slowly, so slowly. But when she comes, she cries.

Falling asleep finally, she realizes that the man in the original memory was not Abraham at all, but Jason Campbell whom she dated ten years ago. And in real life, when she tugged at the waist of his bathing-suit, Jason brushed her hand away as if it were an insect and said, "Don't do that. Someone will see. Are you crazy?"

And so it is in the power of true love to alter everyone and everything that has gone before. All of your former lovers, it seems, are reduced to stand-ins, replaced now in your memories by the figure of the beloved. All of their lips have become his. All of their lips were his all along.

The thought of Abraham is so much with her that often she can't tell whether she's thinking of him or not. She knows this sounds crazy. But he is so much inside of her, that even when she is consciously thinking of other things, she is always aware too of his presence, or now of his absence, which is everywhere. She thinks of all the places they can touch each other when she gets home. They can turn each other inside out.

*...I love you like October...*

Autumn is their favourite season, when the sky is cool blue and the air is a tonic, sharp and invigorating after the humid muzzle of the summer heat. On Saturday, they go walking through the neighbourhood just at that hour when the lights have been lit but the curtains are still open and all the houses are emitting snug squares of yellow light into the deepening afternoon. Carmen knows that half the people inside those houses may well be bored to tears or hollering at each other but they look so contented from the outside that, when she walked like this before she met Abraham, she would be enveloped by a sickening liquid envy running through her like vinegar and, at the sight of lovers walking hand in hand, she would be swamped by a self-pity so caustic that it left her clenching her fists in pure rage, white-knuckled.

Now she and Abraham walk down to the park at the corner, which has been abandoned these cool days by all but the faithful: a woman in a camel-hair coat walking her Cocker Spaniel, a group of half-grown boys in rubber boots and too-small sweaters playing hockey with a ball where the rink will be, another pair of lovers on a green wooden bench eating chocolate doughnuts with their mittens on.

Carmen and Abraham leave the paved pathways and shuffle through the fallen leaves piled so high in places that they are up to their knees and the colours fall away in front of them them like noisy surf. They lie down together and the crispy leaves envelop them. As they put their arms around each other, a woman alone walks past, stares and then averts her eyes. Carmen recognizes this woman as her own former self, fighting her way through another serious Saturday, jamming her fists into her pockets and heading home still alone, with the wasteland of another Sunday yet to come.

On the way home, they gather leaves, carefully selecting the best ones from among the millions under their feet: red, orange, yellow, one maple leaf gone so dark it looks black. At home, Carmen arranges the leaves on lengths of wax paper, places them between sheets of old newspaper, and then presses the whole package beneath the thick volumes of the *Encyclopedia Britannica*.

Abraham, in the living-room, is putting on a tape: *The last time I felt like this / I was in the wilderness / And the canyon was on fire / And I stood on the mountain / In the night / And I watched it burn / I watched it burn / I watched it burn.*

As Carmen watches him from the doorway, he turns for a moment back into the stranger she met at the party, the man she knew nothing about, the man who could change her life if she let him.

At such a moment, unknowingly observed, the beloved

becomes a singular distant miracle, a transcendent untouchable star. At such a moment, the lover is illuminated by the impossibility of love and of loss, galvanized by the immutable possibility of both. At this moment, the lovers may believe they are immortal.

Carmen goes up behind him and drapes her arm around his shoulders, nuzzling her face into his neck. "You smell like the leaves," she says. "You smell like October." He says this is the nicest thing anyone has ever said to him.

*…I love you like a child…*

In the dream, Carmen and Abraham are standing naked face to face but when she reaches out to stroke his neck, the rise of his breastbone, the curve of his hips, he feels like a blank wall covered with glossy white paint.

In the dream, Carmen is pregnant, her round belly slick with sweat and luminous, the way Maureen's breasts were luminous, glistening like mother-of-pearl.

In the dream, Maureen is dead, laid out in a glass coffin covered with flowers and pendulous fruit. The funeral parlour is filled with singing strangers. Maureen says, "Listen. Can you hear me? Listen. Can you hear the sound of my eyes closing, the sound of my breath in your body, the sound of your head coming out from between my legs? Can you hear the singing? Can you hear the celebration?"

When Carmen wakes up sobbing, Abraham takes her in his arms and he says, "Cry, just cry. It's all right to cry."

In his arms like a child, she must give over her fear, all fear all grieving all trust all power, and she must deliver it there into his purified arms. And here is all the faith in the world, all the trust in tomorrow, and the possibility of finding and losing everything, and the rocking of a soul, these souls ecstatic in such sorrow such joy the attainment of all and every extraordinary life.

She is lying facedown on the big bed and he rubs her neck her shoulders, his hands drawing wordless circles into the small of her back, his tongue on her buttocks and the backs of her thighs.

She moves beneath him slowly so slowly and the sweetness runs out of her over his long fingers between her legs between her opening legs inside of her aching where she is aching and he slides in and slides in and slides in moving together sweating and he rubs his wet chest against her trembling back his teeth are on her neck and they are silent so silent they have never loved before in such excellent silence only breath and breathing they are only breathing the room is full of them and she can feel the hot liquid spurting into her and they are blossoms opening in an instant in what could be forever flowers unfurling the petals like pale skin encompassing all the time and they are opening each other opening themselves to the world and there is room enough inside at last for everything room enough for all life new life and the serious suddenness of love and there can be no word for this or if there is a word and if they ever find it there will be nothing left to say and they are moaning and laughing and they will never be ordinary people again.

# The Heart Must from Its Breaking

**Leon Rooke**

I

This is how it happened that morning at the church. Timmons was speaking on a topic that had us all giggling, "What You Do When and If You Get to Heaven and Find It Empty," and we were all there and saw it. How suddenly before Timmons got wound up good the wood doors burst open and there in the sunlight was someone or something, like a fast-spinning wheel made up of gold, though it couldn't have been gold and was probably some funny trick of the light. Anyway, there it was, and beckoning. Must have been beckoning, or calling somehow, because two children got up from their seats at the front and quiet as you please marched right out to him—to him or it—and went through the door, and that was the last any of us ever saw them. Then a second later that other kid—Tiny Peterson was his name—went out too, but his mama was in time to save him. Now I'd lie about it if I could or if I knew how, but it was all so quiet and quick and then over that I wouldn't know how to improve on the actual happening. Out that door and then swallowed up those two kids, and that's all there was to it.

2

He can say that's all if he wants to. Roger Deering sees an affair like this the same way he sees his job, which I would remind you is delivering mail. He drops it through the box, if he can be troubled to come up the path, and then he's gone. What he's left you with don't matter spit to him. But I live in that house now, my sister's house, and I can tell you the story don't end there.

They were my sister's children, Agnes and Cluey. Sister was home in bed sick so I'd taken little Agnes and Cluey to church to hear Timmons give what we hoped would be a good one, and right after the second song, with Timmons hardly begun, Cluey who was on my left stood up and whispered, "Excuse me," and brushed by my knees, then Agnes on my right stood up, mumbled, "Me too" and they went on down the row, scraping by people, getting funny looks, and then going on down the aisle pretty as you please. I thought Cluey had to go to the bathroom. He was always doing that, never going when you told him to and it embarrassed me. But you do get tired of telling a boy to wait wait wait when he's squirming and crossing his legs, trying to hold it in. I don't mean he was doing it that day, I'm only saying that's what I thought he got up for. He'd been nice as pie the whole time, both of them, both while walking along with me to church and while sitting there waiting for Timmons to get primed. So I was in a good mood and bearing them no malice, though they were a long shot from being my favourite nieces and nephews. Sister had been ailing for some while and they were feeling dopey about that, we all were. That was the day Sister died, in fact the very minute, some said. Some said they'd looked at their watches when that door burst open and Cluey and Agnes went out never to be seen again and that very second three blocks over was the very second Sister passed on. It was close, that's all I'm saying, and my skin shivers saying that much, especially when I remember about the blood. But I'm not saying anything about the blood on Sister's window, being content to leave that to the likes of Clayton Eaves who is still dunning me for that ten dollars. I don't like to think of any of it as the truth, for I'm living in Sister's house now and I know sometimes I hear her and that she hears me. Sister dies and her two children disappear the same minute and it does make you think. Though I didn't see any whirling light or gold spinning at the door. I felt a draft, that's all. Like most people with any sense I thought the wind had blown it open, and when people say to me there wasn't any wind that day I just look through them, since any fool knows a gust can come up. Still, it's strange. I can't think what happened to the children. No-one wanted them. I couldn't, and Sister wasn't able. Their daddy couldn't have come and got them because none of us hardly remembered who their daddy was, or wanted to, because even in his best of days he hadn't been what you'd call a solid citizen. He wasn't right in the head, and not much in the body either, and even Sister knew that. So she had her hard times, raising that pair without a hand from him who hadn't been seen I think in nine years when all this happened. No aunts or uncles would have come for them. We don't have kidnappers around here. No, it defies explanation and I've given up trying. When Sister wakes me calling in the night I sit up in bed and answer back and we go on talking that way until her spirit quietens.

I hope Cluey and Agnes are all right, wherever they are, that's all I hope. I don't agree with those who say they're long-since dead, nor those who say they're in heaven either. Timmons might.

3

Sure they're dead. I don't know how, or how come, or why, not having the divine intervention on it, but you can't tell me two children dressed for church and without penny or snotrag between them are going to get out of this town without anyone knowing it. There are just two ways for entering or leaving and that's by the one street that leads off to Scotland Neck at one end and Enfield at the other, and they didn't go either of those ways. Couldn't have, because a hundred people rocking on their porches that fine Sunday when they should have been at Spring Level hearing my sermon on The Empty Hell would have noted their progress and likely turned them around.

So they're dead. Yep, and their bones plucked by now.

Dust to dust and the Lord's will abidith.

Somebody picked them up right off the churchgrounds, I'd say, right there at the door, and spooked them away. Why I don't know. They were ordinary children, no better or worse than most. Funny things go on in this town the same as they do anyplace else and I figure those two are buried this minute down in somebody's cellar or in a backyard where a thousand things hidden go on day in and day out. I've preached till I'm blue in the face, the same as one or two other ministers have, and it's done no good. Not a lick. You can't stamp out the devil's work for he's like a mad dog once he gets going. That's what it was, of course. The old devil keeping his hand in. If it hadn't been those two children it would have been something worse.

We searched the woods, every rock, weed and clover. Nothing. Not a hint.

About that door. I saw *something* but *what* is something else. It wasn't gold, though. It was more like a giant black shadow had spun up over the stairs and filled the doorway. I remember remarking to myself at the time: it's got so dark in here so suddenly I'm going to have difficulty reading my text. I was going to ask Minny at the organ to turn more light on, when Cluey and Agnes got up and distracted me. A second later it was light again. If I'd known what was to happen I would have called out. But who knew? That's how you know it's the devil's work, I say, because you don't. You just don't. You never will.

4

Timmons is right. I was at the organ. I didn't want to be, having a bad cold, but I was. They couldn't get anybody else. My nose was runny, I told them, and I had aches—but so what? "Minny, now Minny, you come on down." So I did. Yet it's the same story every time and nobody ever even bothering to keep up. I've heard cows mooing in a meadow had more rhythm and feeling than the people in that church. But I saw nothing. Saw and heard nothing. No light or gold. No shadow. No children either. It takes a lot in that church to make me turn around. Back trouble, leg trouble, I wore a neck brace for ten years. I keep my back to that lot and that's how I like it. One time a curtain caught fire back there when Orson Johnson—the cross-eyed one—was playing with matches. I looked around then. That's about the only time.

5

My name's Orson, I'm the one she's talking about. What I wished I'd done that day was burn the whole building down. But I didn't and I growed up and I was back there the day those two walked out. Back there whittling on a stick with this Fobisher knife I have. With the wife and hoping it would wind up early, though I knew it wouldn't, so I could go home and have dinner, maybe grab some shut-eye. But, yes, I saw them, and I felt my neck crawl too, before they ever stood up, because something was behind me. Maybe not at the door, but behind me certainly. My skin froze and I remember gripping my wife's wrist I got that scared. I thought it was Death back there, Death calling, and He was going to lay his cold hand over my shoulder and speed me on off. "What date is it?" I asked my wife. "How long we been married?" Now I don't know why I said this, but I know it scared her too, though she just kept shooshing me.

I didn't want to die. Hell, it seemed to me I'd only started living. But "shoosh" she says, so I shoosh. I shoosh right up; I couldn't have said another word anyway. I sat there with my knees knocking, waiting for Death's hand to grab me. Then I see the kids coming down the aisle. They got their faces scrubbed and that ramrod aunt of theirs, Gladys, she had slapped some worn duds on them and got their hair combed. Death's hold on me seemed to loosen a bit and I thought how I might slip out and ask them how their mother was doing—whether she was still in her sick bed or out of danger yet, that sort of thing—maybe slip them a quarter because I'd always felt pity for those kids—and I tried to move, to wiggle out the side and sort of slink to the back door, but what it was I found was I couldn't move. I couldn't stir a muscle. And a second later my hair stood put on my head because a voice was hissing in my ear. "Don't go," it said. "Don't go, Orson, it will get you too"

Though I didn't think then that "too" business was including the kids. I might have got up if I'd known that. I might have headed them off, tried to save them. If anyone could have. I don't know. Oh they're dead, no question of that. I think they were likely dead before nightfall. Maybe within the hour. It's too bad too, especially with their mother going that same day.

6

I felt Orson stiffen beside me. He looked like death warmed over and he started jabbering beside me, shivering so hard he was rattling the whole row. I put my hand down between his legs and pinched his thigh hard as I could but he didn't even blink. He was trying to get out. So I put my hand up where his man parts were and I squeezed real hard and told him to hush up. "Hush up, Orson, stop playing the fool"—something like that. He was freezing cold. He had sweat beads on his brow an inch thick. I brought my heel down on his foot, trying to get him quiet, then I heard him say, "Death, Death, Death." And "Don't go, don't go." He didn't know he was talking. I saw Aaron Spelling, in front of us, lean over and say to Therma that Orson Johnson had a briar in his behind. Therma turned and looked at us. Her mouth popped open. Because Orson was such a sight. I got my hand away real quick from where it was; I just clamped my fingernails into his thigh and kept them there the rest of the service.

Later on we had to get the doctor in, I'd hurt him so and the infection must have lasted a month.

I didn't notice the kids; I had my hands full with Orson.

It was three whole days in fact before I so much as heard of the children gone missing or dead and of their mother's death.

7

I was nursing Tory when she took her final breath. By her bedside I was with a teacup in my lap and watching the window because I thought I'd heard something running around out there. Like a galloping horse it was. But my legs were bothering me, and my sides, so I didn't take the trouble to go to the window and see. I sat sipping my tea, listening to the galloping horse.

It was a day like many another one up to that time except that the house was empty, it being a Sunday, and other than that horse. A few minutes before, when I got up to get my tea, I'd put my head down on Tory's chest. I was always doing that, couldn't help it, because although I've sat with hundreds of sick people I'd never heard a heart like hers. It was like water sloshing around in a bowl; she hardly had no regular heartbeat is what I'm saying. So I'd put my head down over her chest and listen to it slosh like that.

I couldn't see how a human being could live with a heartbeat like that.

The horse it keeps right on galloping. Now and then I'd catch a whir at the window, white-ish, so I knew it wasn't no dark horse. Then all at once my blood just stops, because something has caught hold of me. I look down at my wrist and there's the queerest hand I ever saw. Thin and shrunk and mostly bones. The hand is all it was in that second, and I shrieked. The china cup fell to the floor and broke. Saucer too. Tea I splashed all over me, so I afterwards had to go in and soak my dress in cold water. There were the long red nails though. A vile colour but Gladys said Tory liked it. That she wouldn't feel comfortable in bed, sick like that, without her nails painted, because how would you feel to be in bed like she was and looking like death, in case anybody came in. So let's keep her looking civilized, Gladys said, and one or the other of us kept her nails freshly painted. So after my minute of fright I knew it was Tory's hand, her who hadn't moved a twitch in three months, suddenly sitting up with a grip like steel on my am. It was practically the first sign of life I'd seen in her in the whole time I'd been minding her. She was sitting bolt-up, with her gown straps down at her elbows so her poor little bosom, the most puckered, shrivelled little breasts I ever hope to see, was exposed to the full eyes of the world.

She had her eyes locked on the window.

And there went the horse again, gallop, gallop.

I got hold of myself, got her hand off me and stooped down over her. I was about to say, "Now little lady let's get that gown up over your bosom before you catch your death"—but then that word caught in my throat so I said nothing. And I'm glad I didn't or I might of missed what she said. Her eyes were on fire and she was grabbing at something. At the very air, it seemed to me. "You'll not get my children!" she said. "No, you'll not get them!" Well my skin crawled. I don't know why, don't know to this day. Just the way she was crying it. "You'll not get them, not my Cluey and Agnes!" She was screeching that out now, as frightened—but as brave too—as any soul I hope to see. "*You can't have my children!*" On and on like that. And she was twisting around in bed, flailing her arms, striking at something with her poor little fists. "*No, you can't!*" she said. Then this even worse look come over her face and for the longest time she wasn't making human sounds at all. Half-animal, I thought. Like something caught in a trap. I thought she'd finally bit the noose—that her mind had gone. I kept trying to get that gown up over her breast works—you never knew who would come barging into that house without knocking or breathing a word, even her sister has crept in sometimes and scared me out of my wits. And she's fighting me, not letting me get her back down in the bed. She's scratching and yelling and kicking—her whose legs the doctor claimed was paralyzed—and she's moaning and biting. Then she shrieks, "*Run! Run! Oh children, run!*" And this perfect horror comes over her face, pure agony it is, and torture worse than I've ever known a body to feel. "*No!*" she screams, "*No! Please! Please don't!*" and the next second her breath flies out, her eyes roll up, and she sags down like a broken baby in my arms. I put her head back on the pillow and fluff it some. I pull her straps back up and smooth out her gown over her chest's flatness. I pat the comforter up around her neck. I get her hair looking straight. I close her eyes, first the left then the right just as they say you ought to do, and I root in my purse and dig out two pennies. I go in and wash them off and dry them on my dress, and I put them nicely over her eyes. Then I sit watching her, trembling more than I ever have. Wondering what has gone on and thinking how I'm going to have to tell her sister and those poor children when they come in from the church. Not once giving mind to that broken china on the floor. I reckon I never did. I reckon someone else must have come in and cleared that mess up. Maybe Gladys did. Or maybe not. I plumb can't guess, because one second I'm there sitting looking at my hands in my lap and the next second I'm thinking What about that galloping horse? Because I don't hear it any more. No, it's so quiet you can hear a pin drop. And I hear it too. Pins dropping, that's what I think. This shiver comes over me. I have the funny feeling I'm not alone in the room: that there's me, a dead person and something else. I look over at the bed and what do I see? Well it's empty. Tory ain't there. I hear more of these pins dropping and they seem to be coming from the window so I look there. And what I see is this: it is Tory, come back to some strange form of life, and sliding up over, over the sill and out of that window. That's right, just gone. And I guess I fainted then, that being the first of my faints. The next time I open my eyes my sight is on that window again and this time Tory is coming back through it, sliding along, and her little breasts are naked again, she's all cut up, and blood has soaked through her and she's leaving a trail of it every inch she comes. "Help me, Rosie," she says. Well that's what I'm there for. So I get her up easy as kittens—she hardly weighs an ounce—and I get her back into bed.

"They're safe," she says. I say, "Good." I say a lot of comforting words like that. "Don't let anyone see me like this," she says. "I'm black-and-blue from head to toe." It's the truth too, she sure is. "Have Gladys quietly bury me," she says. "Closed coffin. Can you promise that?" I said sure. She patted my hand then, poor thing, as if I was the one to be comforted. Then she slips away. She slips away smiling. So I get the pennies back on. I straighten the covers. Then I sit back in the chair and faint away a second time. I'm just waking up when Gladys comes in from the church to tell me that Agnes and Cluey have gone and there's been a mighty mess at the church and some are saying the children are dead or gone up to heaven. I pass out my third time. I can't help it. I fold down to the floor like a limp rag and I don't know what else is going on till there is a policemen or a doctor at my elbow. I don't know which.

8

It was me, Sam Clive. Clive, C-L-I-V-E. Officer Sam Clive. I wasn't there in any official capacity. I lived then just two doors down from Tory and that day I felt in my bones how something was wrong. I was out in my yard mowing and this funny feeling come over me. I looked up and it seemed to be coming from her house. It was shut up tight, the house was, but there was this whirring disc in the sky. A flying whatayacallit I at first thought. Anyway, it seemed to sink down in the woods just behind her place. So I strolled over. I saw curtains fluttering in at her sick room window and I was brought up real short by that—because that window had always been closed. Every day, winter and summer, on account of Tory was holding on by such a thin thread. Heart trouble, kidneys, pneumonia—the whole she-bang. I stepped closer, not wanting to be nosey and more because of this eerie feeling I had. Well I saw those curtains were driping blood. It was pouring right off that cloth and down the boards, that blood. And I thought I saw something sliding up over the sill the minute I come up. Flutter, flutter. It was the curtains I guess. Though I don't recollect it being a windy day. But that blood, heck, you can still see where it dribbled down the side of the house, because they never painted it over. They painted the rest of the house, the sister did after she got it, but for reasons known only to them they painted up to the blood and stopped right there. Anyhow, I hurried on over. I looked through the window and there was this fat nurse down in a heap on the floor beside this broken china and Tory in the bed with bright pennies over her eyes.

## 9

I done the paint job. I give the old gal a good price and me and one other, my half-brother who was helping me then, we went at it. White, of course, that was the only colour she'd have. And she wanted two coats, one put on vertical and one crossways. I said why. She said her daddy told her when she was a kid that's how you put paint on if you wanted a thing to stand up to the elements more'n a year or two. I said I'd never heard that. I said Tom Earl, Have you ever heard that and he said No, no he hadn't. She said Well that's how she wanted it and if I wouldn't or couldn't do it or didn't think I was able then she reckoned I wasn't the only painter in town and a lot of them cheaper'n me. Ha! I said. I said it's going to cost you extra. She said I don't see why. I said because Miss Gladys it will take me a good sight longer painting this house the fool way you want it. You can't hardly git no speed painting vertical because the natural way is to go crosswise following the lay of the boards. She said it might be natural to a durn fool like me but that weren't how her daddy done it and I could do it and at the price quoted or I could shove off and go out and stick somebody else. So I got the message. Two coats? I said. Two coats, she said, Hank Sparrow can't you do that neither? I shook my head a time or two. There weren't any way I was going to make one red cent out of it. I'd be doing well just covering wages and gitting the paint paid for. But her sister had passed on and hide nor hair of her kin had been seen, those two children, so I said well it won't hurt me none to do this woman a favour.

I got Tom Earl and him and me took at it. It went right smooth and we did the same top job we always did. Till we got to that window. I brushed the paint over them dark red streaks and said to Tom Earl Well it'll take a second coat but that ought to do her. But when it dried, even after the third and fourth coat, them bloodstreaks were still there same as they were when we started. Tom Earl said Well she ain't going to pay, you know that, until we get these streaks covered over. I looked at him and I said You're right there, you done spoke a big mouthful. And I went out to the truck and got me my tools. Got me my hammer and chisels, my blow torch too: one way or the other I was going to git that blood removed.

Well she comes running. She got her head up in a towel, one shoe off and the other one on and she's dripping water, but still she comes running. What are you doing, what are you doing, she keeps asking, are you going to take hammer to my house or burn it down? Is this what you call painting, she says. So I looked at Tom Earl and he's no help, he just shrugs his shoulders. I look to her and I say I've painted and I've painted and it's still there. What is? she says. Hank Sparrow are you trying to two-bit me? No'm, I say, but there's something peculiar going on here. There sure is, she says, and it's you two with no more sense than a cat has pigeons. Now hold on a minute, I say. So I take her round the house and I show her how we've put on a good seven coats minimum. But still that blood where your sister crawled up over the ledge. You leave my sister out of this, she says. She says, Hank Sparrow I have known you Sparrows all my life and there has never been one of you didn't try to weasel out of work and didn't lie with every breath scored. Now give me that brush, she says.

Tom Earl and me we give it to her. We coat it up good and we wrap a little tissue over the handle so she won't get none on her hand, and we tell her to go to it. We stand back picking our teeth and poking each other, laughing, because one, the way she held that brush in both hands with her tongue between her teeth and bent over like she was meaning to pick up dimes, and two, because we knew it was a lost cause and no way in hell that paint was going to do it.

See there? she said. See there? Now is that covered or isn't it?

Give it a minute, we said. You give them streaks about two minutes and your eyes will pop out.

Well she stood right there with us, insulting us up one side and down the other every inch of the way. But we took it. We said nothing hard back to her. We knowed she was going to get the surprise of her life and be walking over hot coals to beg our pardon. And in two minutes, sure as rainwater, those steaks were back. They looked fresh brand-new, even brighter.

She went back and stood under the tree studying it, thinking her and distance would make a difference.

It's this paint, she said. This is a shoddy paint you're using.

Well we saw there was no end to it. So we got her in the truck between us, her with her hair still up in this green towel, and we drove down to the hardware. She got Henry Gordon pinned in the corner not knowing which way to turn but no matter how hard she pinned him he kept telling her that the paint we had was the best paint made and there weren't none no better including what went on the mayor's own house. I'll see about this, she said. And danged if she didn't call the distributor, long-distance, charging it to Henry. What is the best paint made? she said. And he said the very one we'd put on her house. She slammed down that phone. All right, she said, but Henry Gordon you have sold these two so-called working men a bad mix. I want another. Help yourself, Henry told her. She marches in his stockroom, says eenymeenyminymoe over the cans, and comes out with one. All four of us now go back to her house. She has me git the lid off and she dabs over that blood again, so thick it just trickles down to the ground. We wait. She is now fit to be tied. I have lost a dear sister, she says, and lost my precious niece and nephew, and now you are telling me I've got to live with the curse of this blood?

We said it looked like it. Everyone of us did, jumping right in with it. Because that blood was coming right back up. It was coming up bright as ever.

Well I never, she says.

So we go inside and stand in her kitchen and she gives each of us a co-cola. It surpasses meaning, she said. I don't understand it. I don't guess I'm meant to.

We said Yesmam.

176

All right then, she said, I will just have to leave it there. It's meant to be left there. It's meant to be some kind of sign or signal. A symbol.

We didn't argue with her. I didn't even raise a hand when she said she was holding back $10 paint money because I never finished the house. There was something spooky about that place. All I wanted was to git shut of it. Me and Tom Earl took her cash and I give him some and me and him went out drinking.

## 10

He drank. I didn't because I was only thirteen and the law wouldn't have it. But I knew Cluey, had seen him around, and that Agnes too because she was always at his heels, and I'd heard the stories of how the woman had died and Cluey and Agnes had gone up in thin air. I had beat up some on Cluey, being something of a bully in them days. I had blooded his nose once and left him sobbing. I remember it and know it was him because he threw a rock at me and got me on the kneecap. And because of what he said: "My daddy will git you," he said. I was nice enough not to say, "What daddy?" And I was glad I didn't. Because that night something tripped me up as I was walking home along the dye ditch, and I fell off into that ditch and broke my left leg. It was somebody there all right, that's all I'm saying, and it weren't Cluey or any other thing with two legs. It tripped me up, then it put a hand in my back, and I went tumbling over. I was with Tiny Peterson. He can tell you.

## 11

It's every word true. But what I want to get to is that church. Timmons was being his usual assy self, playing up like he was doing a cameo role for Rin Tin Tin, yammering on about emptiness this and emptiness that, when the wood doors burst open. I was already turned around, trying to smack at a little girl back there, when Cluey come by me. I had my legs up high and he couldn't get past. So he dropped my legs. I'd just got them back up when his little sister tapped my knee. "Excuse me," she said. "Me and him are going out to see my daddy. That's him at the door."

I raised up high in my seat and looked again at that door. People behind me started hissing but I didn't care. There was something in that door all right, but it wasn't hardly human. It didn't have two arms and two legs and it didn't have a face either. But it was beckoning. I saw Cluey and Agnes walk into the thing, whatever it was, and then they simply were not there anymore. There was nothing. I thought it was a vision. Timmons just then got his smart voice back and was saying something about, "Heaven is empty." The empty heaven, something like that. I admit it. Goose bumps rose high on my arm as a kitchen window. I was really scared. Now why I did it I don't know to this day, but I went running out after them. I figured that if maybe their daddy was out there then maybe mine was too and he might save me from my empty heaven. I went flying out. I sped out over everybody's knees and trampled on feet and the next second I was outside in the yard. Cluey and Agnes couldn't have been five seconds in front of me. And what I saw there gave me a chilll I can feel to this minute. There was this woman there in a white gown that was down to her waist so I could see her nipples and these real wizened breasts. I reckon to this day it's why I like big-bosomed women. But what she was doing was struggling with this creature. Creature is what he was, make no mistake about that. She had her arms and legs wrapped around him, pulling and tugging and chewing—pure out-and-out screeching—while the creature thing was trying to throw her off and still hold on to poor Cluey and Agnes who by this time were just bawling. They were just bawling. The creature was dragging them along and that woman was up on the creature's back, riding him, biting into the thing's neck, punching and clawing. Well it let go of the children. It gave a great howl and tore the woman off itself and practically bent her double. I mean it had her with her back across his knees and it was slamming her down all the while she screamed "Run! Run! Oh children run!" And they streaked off. I've never seen nothing tear away so fast. "Run! Run!" she cried. And they did and it was about this time that I heard this galloping, and a great white horse came out of the woods. The prettiest horse I ever will see. It galloped up to the children and slowed down and Cluey swung on its back, then got Agnes up there with him, and that horse took off full-speed, faster than I'd think a horse could. Then gone, just flying. The creature still had the woman. He slammed her down one last time and from where I was, hiding behind the tree, I could hear it: her back snap. *Snap,* like that, and the creature flung her down. It let out a great roar—of hatred, of pure madness at being thwarted, I don't know which—and then it took off too. But in the wrong way, not after the children. It seemed to me, the longer I looked at it run, that the closer it came to having human form. It had arms and legs and a face, though that face looked a million years old and like it hated everything alive.

That's all I saw. My own momma came out then and

fixed her finger over my ear and nearly wrung it off. "Git yourself back in yonder," she said, "and don't you move one muscle lessern I tell you you can. When I git home I mean to put stick to your britches and you are going to wish you'd never been born."

I whimpered some, though not at my ear or at any threats she made. I never told anyone till now. Hell with them.

## 12

The horse came by my place. I was out on the porch rocking away when it come by. Mary was in her chair with peas in her lap, shelling them. It was white, that horse was, it had two riders. They were up in the hills though. They were out a good far piece. There was something unnatural about it, I thought that. About how fast that horse was running, how it didn't get slowed down none by tree or brush. I said to Mary how I'd never seen no horse like that, not around here. Not anywhere else either, I reckon. My dog was down between my legs and he got up and took off after them. About a quarter-hour later he come back whimpering, his tail drawed up under his legs. He went under the house and moaned. It took me two days to git that dog out.

## 13

See that horse? He told me. And he pointed. I went on with my shelling.

Wonder why they don't take the road, I said. Wonder whose it is?

I never saw no children. Didn't see what the dog did either. I didn't look that long. I can't set out on the porch all day like him, watching what goes on. I got my own concerns to look after. Still, it was unusual. In the kitchen washing my hands I found myself staring out at a bluejay in a tree. Was that a horse, I ask myself, or was that a ghost?

## 14

I thought when I went out and tweaked his ear that the sobbing Tiny was doing wasn't on account of that ear. He was snow-white and trembling and it was all I could do to hold him up. If I hadn't been so mad and set in my ways I would have known he'd seen something. It weren't no way for me to behave, whether it's to your own flesh or another's—but my husband had run out on me again and I imagine that had something to do with it.

But I'm sorry for it. I think it was the last time I wrung that boy's ear.

## 15

You are all looking at me. Keep looking, then. You've always come to me with your aches and pains, now you're coming to me with this—is that it? I've told you my end before. I've never held anything back, and I won't now. Yes, I signed the certificate. She'd been slipping a long time and we'd all expected her death. I spent more time than most worrying about her. I said to her one day, "Tory," I said, "my medicines are doing you no good. I know you are in terrible pain all day and we both know you haven't got long. If you've a mind to, and want me to, and realize I am only raising this issue because I am aware of your misery, then I could give you something to help you go out easy and gentle and without the smallest pain."

She always told me she'd think on it. She'd let me know, she said. Then one day, after I'd given her every painkiller I could and none of it was helping her the slightest bit, I raised the question again.

"I'd like to go off, doctor," she said, "in a nice and swoony dream just as you describe. But I can't go yet. I've got to hold on for my children's sake because I know one day he is coming back. I've got to stay and save them from him, if I can."

I knew, of course, who she was talking about. You can't live here as long as I have without knowing that. But I said: "Tory, if he *does* come back, we will take care of his hide. You don't have to worry about his harming your kids."

"You don't understand," she said. "There will not be a single thing a living soul can do. No," she said, "I will have to take care of this myself, if I'm able. But I thank you."

I didn't mean to divulge this. Though I don't see how it alters anything. It tells us something of the spirit she had, I suppose, and confirms the love and concern she had for that boy and girl. The rest of it I'd discount. I never saw evidence of anything to the contrary while I was in medical school. Nor since, either. Yes, I signed the death certificate. You know as I do that it was a natural death. The heart couldn't any longer do its job. Yes, she was black-and-blue all over. Yes, there was blood on the curtains, and not merely her own blood either. I ran a test. The report came back to me and an idiot at the laboratory had scribbled on it, "Please provide more information."

Well, I didn't. I wasn't about to let myself be made a fool

of up there.

I'm done. Let Tory and her children rest in peace, I say. Let these stories stop right here.

LINDA SVENDSEN grew up in Vancouver and has recently been teaching at the Creative Writing department at the University of British Columbia. Her work has appeared in *Second Impressions* and in several previous editions of *Best Canadian Stories*. Her first collection of stories is forthcoming from Random House.

PATRICIA SEAMAN lives in Toronto. Her first novel, *Hotel Destine*, was published by gynergy books in 1989. Her stories have appeared in the anthology *Imagining Women* and in various periodicals including *Borderlines, (f.)Lip, Fuse* and *Parachute*.

TIMOTHY FINDLEY received the Governor General's Award for his novel *The Wars* and is the author of numerous books, the most recent being *Not Wanted on the Voyage* and *Stones*. He lives near Cannington, Ontario.

GEORGE BOWERING was brought up in rattlesnake country in the South Okanagan. He is the author of nine books of fiction. His novel *Harry's Fragments* has just been published by Coach House Press and he is now working on a new collection of stories.

ROHINTON MISTRY is the author of *Tales from Firozshah Baag*. His stories have appeared in various periodicals and anthologies including *Coming Attractions 4*. He lives in Brampton, Ontario and is working on a second collection of stories and a novel.

DEBBIE HOWLETT was born in Montreal in 1964. Her stories have appeared in a number of Montreal-based literary magazines, including an anthology published by

Nu-Age Editions entitled *Passions & Poisons*. She is currently finishing her MFA degree at the University of British Columbia and is the editor of PRISM International.

DIANE SCHOEMPERLEN is originally from Thunder Bay. She lived in Canmore, Alberta for ten years and now lives in Kingston, Ontario. She has published four collections of short fiction: *Double Exposure, Frogs and Other Stories, Hockey Night in Canada* and *The Man of My Dreams*.

LEON ROOKE spent many years in British Columbia and now lives in Eden Mills, Ontario. He is the author of several books, most recently *A Good Baby* and has appeared frequently in *Best Canadian Stories*.

*Acknowledgements:* "Stardust" by Linda Svendsen and "The More Important Things" by Rohinton Mistry originally appeared in *Canadian Fiction Magazine.* "The Duel in Cluny Park" by Timothy Findley, copyright © by Pebble Productions Inc., was first published in *Toronto Life.* "Staircase Descended" by George Bowering first appeared in *West Coast Review.* "The Heart Must From Its Breaking" by Leon Rooke was first published in *Exile.*

ISBN 0 88750 817 0 (hardcover)
ISBN 0 88750 818 9 (softcover)
ISSN 0703 9476

Cover art by Mendelson Joe
Book design by Michael Macklem

Printed in Canada

PUBLISHED IN CANADA BY OBERON PRESS